Sharecropper's Son

Don Cusic

Sharecropper's Son

© 2011 by Don Cusic

Brackish Publishing
P.O. Box 120751
Nashville, TN 37212

All rights reserved. Printed in the United States of America. No Part of this book may be reproduced in any manner whatsoever without written permission except in the case of brief quotations embodied in critical articles and reviews.

Cover Design & Layout by
Wendy Mazur
theoddballgroup.com
Cover Illustration by
Adam Courville

Production Coordinator
Jim Sharp
SharpManagement@Comcast.net

One

Aunt Tootie yesterday come barrelin' down the road in her blue Ford and pulled up in our yard. She'd raised a rooster tail of dust that was coming back down like each little speck had a parachute on it. Mama always said "A cloud of dust, a streak of blue and it's hi ho Tootie." That's the way it was yesterday.

Aunt Tootie come to tell us that Granny Gregory had been carried off to the hospital in an ambulance. Granny was coming back from Lynnville and was almost home when she realized she'd forgot to pick up something for Uncle Roadkill at the feed store so she raised up both of her hands. When she did that her car run into the ditch.

Granny only learned to drive two years ago, after Granddaddy Gregory had died; before then she'd never drove a car in her life. Uncle Roadkill taught her but she had to put four or five pillows on her seat so's she could see out the windshield.

It was lucky that me and Daddy was at the house already. We had come in from the fields to get some water so Daddy, Mama, me and Charlene, my sister, all piled in our car and went over to the Lynnville Hospital where Granny was. Aunt Tootie had to swing by her own house to check on her kids, she said, and then she'd come on to the hospital.

When we got to the hospital Uncle Roadkill was already there. So was Uncle T-Bone, Uncle Soup and Aunt Fussie, and Uncle Bubba and Aunt Ilene. You might as well know right now that Daddy's family's got nicknames for each other. Roadkill's real name is Orville but he got his nickname cause when he's driving he'll put a car in a ditch just to hit some animal in the road. He loves running over possums, squirrels, dogs, or cats. Anything in the road, really. So that's why they call him Roadkill.

Uncle T-Bone's real name is Oswald but he likes steaks. Uncle Soup's real name is Oliver but he's called "Soup" cause he likes to soup up cars. That's when you fix the engines so they can race and put stripes on 'em and stuff. Bubba's real name is Orvon but he's the youngest, so he's always been called Bubba. Daddy is called Catnap cause he likes to catnap. His real name is Othello. Granny said she named him Othello because she wanted him to have a Biblical name. She thought some of the other names were Biblical too. There are two other brothers. Uncle Odom is in the Air Force, stationed in Germany, and Uncle Oscar lives in Florida and works on air conditioners. There's no girls in that family.

Granny and Uncle Roadkill live together on a farm about four miles from our farm. Daddy and Uncle Roadkill work together, helping each other on the two farms. Uncle T-Bone and Uncle Bubba both work for the telephone company and Uncle Soup works for the William P. Bretton Plumbing Company fixing sinks, toilets, pipes and stuff. Aunt Tootie is Mama's sister and she's married to Uncle T-Bone, Daddy's brother. So their kids and us are double first cousins.

Aunt Tootie got to the hospital about a half hour after all the rest of us had got there. By that time everybody was in a turmoil over Granny Gregory cause she'd been taken to the emergency operating room on one of those real narrow beds as soon as she arrived. That had been about an hour ago. Since then nobody could find out nothing. Everybody had lit up a cigarette and the hospital room was so full of smoke it looked like Granny's car had been sitting inside there running.

Aunt Tootie finally stopped a nurse and asked about Granny—her real name is Olivia Mae Gregory—and the nurse just smiled and said, "Oh yes, she and the baby are doing fine" and then left. Well, none of us could figure out how Granny got pregnant at the age of sixty-two without a husband. Aunt Tootie kept saying "The Lord works in mysterious ways" and then she'd say, "What is she going to do with the baby?"

A little while later another nurse come out and didn't say nothing to us but went over to the main desk and told the nurse sitting there loud enough for all of us to hear that "The old woman they brought in from the car wreck has died. We need to notify her family." That made things even worse than they was cause then Aunt Tootie started crying and saying, "Who's going to raise the baby?"

Everybody else was real quiet except the women folk who was all crying. Finally, Uncle Roadkill said, "I reckon we better call the funeral home and make arrangements." So Roadkill and Uncle Soup went over to the pay telephone and called the Lynnville Funeral Home cause they was the ones that buried Granddaddy Gregory. By this time it was almost seven o'clock and we'd all been there since around six. Granny's accident had happened near about five o'clock.

Uncle Roadkill and Uncle Soup come back from the pay phone and said they had an appointment at the Funeral Home for eight o'clock to pick out Granny's casket and decide when she'd be buried. Aunt Tootie asked Mama and Aunt Fussie whether they should call an adoption agency or not for the baby. Aunt Fussie didn't like that idea at all. She said the baby should be raised by family cause that was the right thing to do. It wasn't right for a baby to be raised by strangers who was no blood kin. Mama didn't agree and said it would be best to find a couple that wanted a baby and give it to them. They'd appreciate it more and give it a good home.

Well, that baby started a big argument. Aunt Fussie said she and Soup couldn't raise it cause they already had three—the twins J. T. and Randy and a daughter, Shirley. Aunt Ilene said they couldn't raise it neither. There was no room at their house for a baby and Aunt Tootie said she already had her hands full with her own brood. Mama was never even considered cause she had let it be known from the git go that she thought the baby should be put up for adoption.

Aunt Tootie said, "Supposin' a nice, young couple adopts it, then moves away? It would lose all contact with its blood kin. And that ain't right."

Mama said, "It wouldn't know we was relatives anyway. When somebody gets adopted they think the people that raise 'em are their real parents."

Aunt Fussie said "You should always know who your kin is" but Mama said, "Why? So they can borrow money?"

That started another argument about money. Everybody agreed they didn't have any extra money to lend to some stranger they hadn't seen since birth. They even argued about what this stranger would want to borrow money for. Most agreed it would be for a car but then Aunt Tootie said, "Suppose some smart people adopted it and then it came to us to pay for a college education? We can't afford to pay for some stranger's college education just because it's got some Gregory blood in it."

Aunt Fussie said that nobody in our family was smart enough to go to college and she didn't see that ever changing but car insurance kept going up and that could cost a bundle, especially if it was a boy. That was the first time anybody thought about whether the baby was a boy or girl.

That got Tootie, Fussie, Ilene and Mama talking about who had any baby stuff left from raising their own kids when Uncle Roadkill says, "It's almost eight o'clock. We better get over to the funeral home and pick out a casket." Uncle Soup said "I'll go with you" and those two left.

Aunt Tootie said she was getting right tired and wanted to go home but, "I'd hate to leave before I knew if it was a boy or a girl." Then she said, "Maybe we can go upstairs to the maternity ward and look at it through the window." Bubba, Ilene and Fussie all decided they'd like to go up and peek at the baby through the window, too. Mama said our family was all going home cause it was past time for supper.

That's when Granny walked out into the hospital lobby where we all was. Soon as she did, Aunt Tootie said, "Where's the baby?"

"What baby?" said Granny.

"Didn't you just have a baby?"

Granny looked at her kinda funny and said, "Babies come after you get pregnant from a husband."

Aunt Fussie shouldn't a said it but she did anyway. She said, "Having a husband don't mean nothing nowadays. Girls get pregnant all the time."

Granny shot back, "I'm sixty-two years old so I ain't no girl. And when I got pregnant, I had a husband."

Aunt Tootie dropped her pocketbook right on the floor and said out loud, "You been pregnant for over two years? Ever since Granddaddy died? How come you never showed?"

"What in the world are you talking about, Tootie?" said Granny. "I'm not pregnant. I run in the ditch. There's a difference."

Then Granny says, "Why are all you here? I only needed one of you to pick me up. Where's Roadkill?"

Bubba said, "He went over to the funeral home to pick out your casket."

Granny looked at Bubba hard and says, "And just who does he think will cook his dinner if he buries me?"

Bubba got real flustered and said, "We thought you was dead."

"Do I smell that bad?" said Granny. "Who told you I was dead?"

"Some nurse," said Daddy. "That's how we learned about the baby too. Some nurse said you and the baby was doing fine. Then another nurse come out and said you was dead. So Roadkill and Soup went to pick out your casket while Tootie and them was all deciding what to do with the baby."

"Well I'm not dead and I don't have no baby," said Granny. Then she looked straight at me and said, "Compton Gregory, tuck in your shirt."

"Yes'm," I said.

"I wish he'd do somethin' I told him to," said Mama. "He just ignores me."

"Yes'm," I said.

"I'm tired," said Granny. "And it's past supper time and I ain't got nothin' fixed. So let's go home,"

"We'd better go over the funeral home first and let Roadkill and Soup know you're all right," said Daddy.

"What funeral home did they go to?" asked Granny.

"Lynnville," said Mama.

"Why'd they go over to that Lynnville Funeral Home?" said Granny. "They did a sorry job of buryin' my husband and charged me an arm and a leg to do it. I don't want to pay them another red cent. They ain't gettin' any more money from me."

"Granny, what happened in your operation?" said Aunt Tootie. "Did they sew you up or what?"

"Well, they wheeled me into the operating room," said Granny. "But as soon as I got inside the door they rushed in another woman having a baby. So they pushed me off to the side while she had her baby. Then as soon as that baby come out they wheeled in somebody else and looked at 'em, said they was dead, and all those doctors and nurses just walked out. Left me back there by myself. I laid there for a while, took a little nap, woke up and come on out. So here I am. Let's go."

We all went out to the parking lot and Granny got in Bubba and Ilene's car and we all went over to the funeral home. We walked in just as Roadkill and Soup were shaking hands with the casket salesman. There was a bright blue casket with yellow silk lining open on rollers right beside them.

"Don't tell me you picked out that ugly casket for me, Roadkill," said Granny as she walked in. "It doesn't look very sturdy either. I want somethin' that will keep out water."

I could tell that Uncle Roadkill just about browned his bermudas when he saw her. He stared at her for about a minute with his mouth half open and then he said, "Where's the baby?"

"Tootie's got it," said Granny. "Now let me see those caskets."

The salesman took her by the arm and led her into a whole room full of caskets. Granny spent about a half hour in there looking them over. Finally, she picked out a steel gray one with red velvet lining that was extra reinforced. "That's the one I like," said Granny. "It's got a rubber seal around it so it'll keep out water."

"But it's four thousand nine hundred and ninety-nine dollars," said Roadkill.

"Don't you remember I've got a five thousand dollar life insurance policy?" said Granny. "Well, that's how I want it spent."

Because of Granny's accident and all we didn't get home until after nine o'clock last night. But that's how we all learned what kind of casket Granny Gregory wanted to be buried in.

Two

Today was a real monumental day for me. They had the Talent Show at school today and I got up and sang on it.

The Talent Show is a big deal at our school cause it only happens once a year, although they have other musical performances during the rest of the year. There's always a Christmas program and a Spring Concert, but that's the Chorus. We have a play every year, too, but this Talent Show is the one time when somebody who ain't the chorus type can get up and sing in front of the other kids at school.

All you have to do to be on the Talent Show is sign up in the Principal's office, which I did last week. You can sign up in your Home Room but I don't trust my teacher cause last year I signed up but somehow I never got on. My home room teacher blamed it on the Principal's office, said somebody forgot something or whatever. So I didn't take me no chances this year. They's always talking about doing auditions and not letting just anybody get up no matter what but every year there's just enough people signed up so they just put on whoever wants to be on. That's what happened this year. So I showed up and then got up when it was my turn.

When I got up to sing my mouth was so dry it felt like a cave packed with a load of cotton. There wasn't a speck of water in my mouth and when I tried to swallow it was like trying to gulp a bucket of sand. My hands were sweaty and it didn't really feel like I was all there, felt more like I was circling the scene and there was this big buzz all around me like some kind of flying saucer landing.

I was third on the program and the whole school was there watching. I didn't tell nobody at home I was going to do this. When Daddy asked why I was taking my guitar to school this morning I just said some of the other boys wanted to see it. "Well, don't let nobody steal it" was all he said.

Each contestant got to do two songs on the Talent Show. My first song was an old country tune, "The Wild Side of Life." I'd practiced on that song a thousand times but danged if I could remember a single word when I walked up to the microphone in the middle of the stage. I knew it was in the key of D and that's where my fingers were on the guitar neck but it didn't feel like I could move my fingers. They was frozen and I thought I'd probably have to play that whole song in one chord. I knew it wouldn't sound exactly right but it woulda taken a chisel to undo my fingers and I didn't have one handy.

I was having second thoughts about my song, too. All the kids in class except me liked rock'n'roll. Except Tommy Junior Morgan, who liked country music if he was away from school. The rest of 'em always let me know plain and clear that they hated country music. But I love it and that's all I ever play.

Actually, when I was sitting in my chair waiting my turn I was wondering how long it would take me to learn a Beatles song for this crowd. I thought about that while I was on the side of the stage just before I walked on, too, but since I was due to go on as soon as the girl on stage quit tap dancing, I knew there wasn't enough time to learn no new song. Even if the song was real simple. And Beatles songs have chords in 'em I've never exactly figured out yet or even heard of.

I remember being introduced and I remember walking out on the stage and standing in front of the mike and then I went on automatic pilot. I couldn't think of the words but I started strumming my guitar and then I opened my mouth and "You wouldn't read my letter if I wrote you" come tumbling out. That's the first line of that song and the rest of the words just followed along automatic.

I sang "Wild Side of Life" and played it all the way through to the end but I still don't know how. I remember starting and I remember finishing but I don't remember much in between. Soon as it was over I could hear a few people applauding. I never looked up from the neck of my guitar. I put my fingers in the C chord position, cleared my throat, and started on my second song, "King of the Road."

Right after I started that song I felt a whole lot better. The first song was an old country song and some of those kids had never even heard of it, but "King of the Road" was on the radio. It wasn't a rock'n'roll song but ole Roger Miller was singing it on the radio right next to the Beatles. As soon as I started that song the kids recognized it and started whooping and clapping. That gave me some confidence and for the first time I looked out in the audience. I probably shouldn't a done that cause all those people looking back like to scared the living daylights right outta me. So I looked down at my guitar again real quick and for the rest of the song I'd just sneak a peek at the audience now and then. They seemed to like that song and by the time it was finished I felt like I was puttin' it across real good.

When I finished I could hear a lot of applause and there was a warm flush that come over me. Right then it just felt right being on that stage and singing but I did a quick bow and got off that stage for the next act. At the side of the stage I put my guitar back in its case and when I got up one of the teachers smiled and said something or other to me that sounded like "nice job." Also, one of the girls dressed up like a ballerina gave me a weak smile when I walked past her carrying my guitar. Mostly I just kept my head down and went out front and sat down in the chairs they saved for the contestants and stayed there until it was all over. Which took a long time. I was the third act and there was fifteen on that day.

That was the first time I ever sang in public.

I watched the rest of the show but I don't remember seeing nothing. All I did was think about how I did, which sometimes I felt was all right and other times I felt wasn't too good. Three teachers judged the contest and they gave prizes for first, second and third. I didn't get a prize. That caused me to decide that I hadn't done too good, so when it was all over I picked up my guitar and headed out to the school bus where I got on and sat looking out the window all the way home. Nobody said nothing to me except Tommy Junior Morgan who wanted me to take out my guitar and play something. But I wouldn't. He wanted to hear some Elvis songs.

Finally, the bus got to Wendell's Store, which is where my sister Charlene and I get off, and we got out and walked the mile to get home.

After we got off she said "I thought you did pretty good" but I didn't know whether to trust her or not so I didn't say nothing. Then she said "Girls always like guys who can sing and play a guitar" but I thought that was hogwash. I didn't feel like I played and sang good enough for girls to get excited. Except for dumb ones. Actually, I wanted to believe her but somehow I couldn't bring myself to do it so as soon as I got home I put my guitar in my room and changed into my work clothes and then headed over to the barns where Daddy was working.

Three

It's June and school will be out in a couple of days and then there's the whole summer until school starts again. Not that I get to just lollygag around or anything. When you're a farmer there's always work to do and it never all gets done so you never get to the point where you can kick back and do nothing. Even when you do nothing you always know there's stuff you could be doing, but sometimes you just get tired or feel lazy or think maybe things can wait a bit. I figure the world won't stop turning if I just cool my heels or sit a spell now and then, so I do.

The school bus stops at Wendell's Store every morning to pick up me and Charlene and every afternoon to let us off. Wendell's is a General Store that has a little bit of everything. We get our bread and milk and most of our groceries there. There's a glass covered candy counter and some odds and ends— stuff like clothes and hats and knick knacks and hardware like nails and hinges and everyday stuff you always need. The Post Office used to be at one end of the store but now it's got its own building about a hundred yards away.

The store's run by two brothers, Frog and Tadpole Wendell. Their real names are Howard and Clarence but they been called Frog and Tadpole ever since they's kids. Tadpole is big and fat while Frog is tall and skinny. Tadpole always has a half smoked cigar stuck in his mouth and likes to play the Big Wheel. Always has a big wad of money in his pocket. Daddy said that one time Tadpole pulled the big wad out and peeled off a dollar bill and there was a corn cob left. He'd put that corn cob in his pocket to make it look like he had more money but his bluff got called that time.

In the back of the store is a barroom. Actually two barrooms, one for the whites and one for the colored. I've been in the colored bar, which isn't normally allowed, but I went in the morning while waiting for the school bus when nobody else was in there.

The bar is actually one big room with a dividing wall but the bar itself runs across both places so one bartender can work both sides of the room. The jukebox is on the white's side and so is the pool table but there's two card tables over on the colored's side.

Wendell's Store is on the main road of Clayton, and this road runs all the way down to St. John's Bay, where it dead ends. The store is twelve miles from Lynnville, which is the county seat. You might say Clayton is a suburb of Lynnville. From Wendell's Store another paved road runs up towards Boscoe and on this road is the baseball field and then the Post Office. You go up this paved road just past the Post Office and turn left on a gravel road and that's the road that goes to our farm. This gravel road runs about half a mile through woods on both sides, then there's a field on the right and then our house. If you go past our house the road winds past some more fields and then there's our barns. Mr. Bloodworth's mansion, which sits high and mighty looking out over St. John's Bay, is past our barns a little ways. He owns our farm.

It's a little over a mile walk from Wendall's to my house but I do it pretty quick. Sometimes it gets a little tough if I have to carry a bunch of school books but that ain't a problem now cause school is almost out so there's no homework.

Four

This place is called Clayton, Virginia and Wendell's Store is pretty much it for shopping. In fact, if you had to ask where Clayton is you'd just point to Wendell's Store. The rest of the place is just farms and houses except for the baseball field, Post Office and another bar. If you're looking for excitement that's about it for downtown Clayton.

This is the northern part of Virginia, right across the Potomoc River from Maryland and it's real flat and there's water all around—bays and rivers and such. People here are either watermen or farmers and I've got a little of both in my blood. My Daddy's family is farmers but Mama comes from watermen. Down the main road of Clayton about another five miles past Wendell's Store to where it dead ends is a place called The River View Tavern, which used to be a general store and barroom. Now it's just a barroom and place for watermen to sell their crabs, oysters or fish. It's the only other business establishment in the area. It's on the water and boats come up to buy gas and fishing bait. The owner makes money from the summer tourists in their boats and from the watermen when he takes the crabs, oysters and fish and sells them to restaurants.

My Grandpa Hevington, who was my Mama's Daddy, used to own The River View Tavern. He also ran bootleg whiskey dressed like a priest. Actually, he'd quit running it by the time I come along but he ran it all during Prohibition. He drove this big old tanker car but he'd dress up like a priest. When he made his runs to Richmond and back there'd be road blocks but he'd always say "Bless you boys" or something like that and the policemen on the roadblocks would always say "Hello Father, how are you today" and just wave him through.

Grandpa Hevington used to always check with the nuns at the convent to see if any of them needed a ride to Richmond cause it helped if there was some nuns in the car with him. Less likely to get stopped by the police at a roadblock. He didn't really dress like a priest in the strictest sense but he wore one of those starched white collars backwards and a black suit and sorta looked like one. Those nuns never suspected they was riding in a car that was carrying moonshine.

Everybody called him Captain Dan, although the way they said it made it sound more like Cap'n Dan. He stayed drunk for twenty-seven years. It was only just before he died that he sobered up but he wasn't no laying down sorry drunk or nothing like that. He drank all day long but he kept working. Now his three sons are a different story. Rayburn isn't a drunk in the strictest sense but he lives in a world all his own. Used to tell prophecies and all that. Samford, who we call Uncle Sam, isn't never around too much cause he's in the Merchant Marines, but every now and then he'll get sent back home to dry out and be around for awhile. When he first gets back he'll just lay in a dark bedroom in Grandma Hevington's house and be rather surly and put-off. You aren't supposed to bother him or mess around with him then, but later on as he gets sober, he's pretty fun to be around and a likeable sort. There's always stories you hear about him having a wife and family in some port or other and even some pictures of a Japanese wife. I've probably got cousins all over this world I don't even know about. I haven't seen Uncle Samford in a couple of years.

The other son, Uncle Elton, is the town drunk.

Actually, Uncle Elton is in the Merchant Marines too, but he operates different from Uncle Samford. Uncle Elton signs up on a Merchant Marine ship and has all his checks sent home to his sister, my Aunt Noodles. He'll stay stone cold sober the whole trip and be gone for a couple of months, then he'll get home, collect all those checks and get a room at the motel in Lynnville and start drinking. He'll stay drunk until the money runs out and then he'll sober up. Then he'll go get on another Merchant Marine ship and do it all over again. He's done that for years and years.

Uncle Elton is the funniest man on the face of the earth. In Lynnville he'll get lubricated and then go into each store on the square. He knows just about everybody and enjoys entertainin' 'em. He'll go into a store, put on a little show and tell stories and stuff and people can't stop laughing. I mean he is always funny. No matter what anybody else says he'll always say something to top them. People buy him drinks to hear him talk and he keeps getting funnier but sometimes he'll drink a little too much and by late afternoon he'll be passed out on the sidewalk. Then Mama or one of her sisters will have to go over and get him. Mostly it used to be Aunt Tootie or Aunt Noodles cause we didn't have a telephone but a couple of years ago we got a telephone and since then Mama started getting called. We'll go over to town and find Uncle Elton, passed out in an alley or on the sidewalk, and get him into the car. Generally we take him home and put him in my bedroom, which means that's lost to me for awhile. But usually Uncle Elton just sleeps off an episode and then goes back to town. Ain't nothing you can do about it, though Lord knows everybody's tried to talk sense and sobriety into him. At least he's friendly and funny and gets along with everybody so he never causes any bad trouble.

Five

Uncle Elton was married once but his wife ain't around. I don't know where she is or why we never see her. Everybody said she was real pretty but then she left him and that's what got him drinking heavy. She come from Baltimore I think and he met her when he was in the Army during the War. They had a son named Robert, who would be my cousin and who was born the same year I was, 1948, except I was born October 31 and he was born in March. I only met him once and that was when Grandpa Hevington died in 1955 so I don't remember much about him. I haven't seen him in years and don't even know where he lives. I do know that grown-ups whisper about him now and then but nobody ever tells me nothing or what for.

When the family gets together the kids are supposed to lay low and go off somewhere and play. That used to be a lot more fun than just sitting around and listening to grown ups talk but I'm 16 now and finishing up my junior year in high school. It seems like I oughta be able to sit at the same table as the grown ups during dinner now instead of in another room with the kids. And I ought to be let in on more stuff. Two of the boys in Mama's family died young. Matthew was only six when he got a tetanus shot at school, then he got lockjaw and died. From then on Grandpa and Grandma Hevington wouldn't let any of their kids get any kind of shots. Whenever school officials came out and insisted on it they just told the officials what happened to Matthew and the school officials left them alone cause none of those officials could guarantee it wouldn't happen again. Right at the head of Matthew's grave is a little white marble lamb. It looks so innocent and every time I go to that graveyard I look at it and just can't believe a little six year old boy could die that way and be buried there. But I never cry cause he died before I was born so I never knew him.

The other son who died young was Mitch. He shot himself dead right after Christmas in 1950. If there is one big mystery in our family, that's it.

Mitch had been in the Army and had gotten out early. He was pretty young and was the favorite of all the girls in the family. That family was kinda funny cause none of my aunts on the Hevington side would so much as even touch a drop of liquor while the boys stayed drunk all the time. That was the way it was with Grandpa and Grandma Hevington too. She wouldn't touch a drop and he couldn't drop the touch. Grandma used to say that if there was a nip in the air, Grandpa would drink it. He nipped all the time. Actually, Grandma couldn't hold any liquor. One time Grandma was thirsty like crazy and there was Grandpa's drink so she poured it all out and just ate the ice and got drunk. Grandma couldn't tolerate any kind of hard stuff.

Nobody ever sat me down and explained Mitch's killing himself to me full and plain. From what I've been able to piece together Uncle Mitch and one of his running buddies, Little Herbert Hoover, (whose family name was Hoover so he had been named for a President cause his family thought they should take advantage of the fact there'd been a Herbert Hoover in the White House even though they had voted for Roosevelt) had been out drinking or running around or something the day after Christmas. Then just before dark Uncle Mitch went back home and got his shotgun and went down to a creek about a half mile away from his house and shot himself dead.

I've heard the women folk on that side of the family say that Little Herbert told them he thought things were fine with Mitch, although they'd argued a little bit here and there. But mostly the family says it's all just a great big mystery and nobody will ever know what really happened. They also say it's not polite to keep asking about things like that and the dead should be left alone to rest in peace.

Nobody ever thought Little Herbert was to blame but he's stayed drunk the rest of his life. He's one of those crawling do nothing slurred speech drunks. Uncle Elton joined the Navy right after that, which was pretty unusual because that meant he served in both the Army and Navy during his life. That's why Uncle Elton wasn't seen again until Grandpa Hevington died. I think Elton must've taken it pretty hard cause he and Mitch was real close.

Little Herbert and Uncle Elton started to hang out and drink together after Grandpa died cause Uncle Elton got out of the Navy after the funeral and moved back. They stay in an old boat house just below The River View Tavern. Last Thanksgiving Aunt Tootie went to find Uncle Elton to come over for dinner and found him and Little Herbert at the boathouse cooking up a pot of stew. Man, that pot had everything in it. I hadn't never seen nothing like it before and I ain't never seen nothing like it since. There was hot dogs and cans of soup and Lord knows what all. That was their Thanksgiving dinner and they said that and a bottle was all they needed. Wouldn't come over for dinner, just wanted to stay there at the boat house. Aunt Tootie went back to the house where everybody was gathered and got them each a plate full of food and brought it to 'em. That was the best thing to do cause drunks don't like to sit through a whole dinner with sober people.

Six

Well it's June, like I said, and about a month ago—it was on May 1, I remember cause that's Charlene's birthday—Daddy told me he needed me to help him more on the farm. It was after we had eaten the birthday cake and ice cream and were sitting on the porch. He never exactly said times was hard but he did point out that last year's crop didn't pay much.

It was dry all last summer, real dry, and the tobacco just didn't grow like it should've. There wasn't no rain nowhere even though we prayed for it every single Sunday. Prayed for rain at special times too but that didn't do no good either. By August it didn't look none too good. None of the crops amounted to much—no ears on the corn, the tobacco real small and pitiful. And every day I could see my Daddy getting more and more worried.

I'm sixteen now and can shoulder the load of a man. I helped a lot anyway, but now I'll have to help even more and get serious about it. That's what Daddy said, "You need to get serious about work now." Daddy always said I loved to have fun too much to ever amount to much. Said until I got serious about things I'd never amount to much but I never liked being serious. It took too much effort and wasn't no fun.

Farming's a big gamble at best. You work up your land and plant your seeds and cultivate and do everything right and if it don't rain at the right time nothing matters. If it rains too little the crops won't grow enough and if it rains too much the crops might wash out and drown and you've lost everything. If it rains at the wrong time you're sunk again cause grown crops will blow over in the mud and there ain't nothing you can do about that either.

One year we had a good crop of tobacco about ready for cutting in late August with the blooms still on them. You want to keep them blossoms on as long as possible to get those top leaves to spread out and then just before cutting you walk down the rows and cut those blooms off. Topping the tobacco it's called. Well, a big storm come up quick and fast one day and by supper time it looked like the end of the world with big dark heavy clouds covering the sky like it was midnight and the wind coming fast and hard. Me and Daddy had to miss supper that night cause we was going up and down those rows with a pocket knife topping that tobacco as fast as we could.

Usually when you top tobacco you reach down kinda low but this time we just walked as fast as we could and cut those tops out up high. Wasn't time enough to do it right. We topped until it was so dark we couldn't see and the rain was coming down hard and fast so we finally had to go back to the house. My daddy was worried big time and when we got home he couldn't eat and just looked out the window. When I went to bed he was still up.

That night the whole crop blew down. Next morning we went out and looked and it would'a made you sick, all that tobacco laying in those fields covered with mud. Fields so muddy you couldn't get a tractor and wagon in 'em to cut that tobacco and haul it out and maybe try to save some of it. We walked through those fields all day and tried to get that tobacco to stand up but it was pretty useless. The whole crop was just gone. Corn and soy beans took a beating too.

That's farming for you. Everything depends on the weather and there ain't nothing more unpredictable than the weather. Like I said, you can be the best farmer in the whole wide world, do everything right at the right time and all that, but if it don't rain when you need it to your crops will suffer and you won't make it as a farmer.

Course, you can't win at farming on either side. Suppose it does rain at all the right times with the right amount. Well, if it goes that way for you then it rains like that on everybody else's crops too so everybody looks good with fine crops. But when it comes time to sell nobody gets much money cause the buyers say there's plenty of good stuff so they don't pay much money. Plenty of supply cuts the demand for good crops and that drives prices down for everybody. If it's a bad crop then buyers say they can't pay much cause it ain't worth much. They want quality. So bad crops drive the prices down for everybody, too. Heckuva way to make a living. With farming you always feel so helpless and at the mercy of everything. If the weather ain't working against you then the buyers are and there ain't nothing you can do about either one. You just gotta take what you're given and make do.

I'll tell you one thing, though. The farmers that stick with it really love what they do. Love that land and being outside. You get a bunch of farmers together and they'll talk about the weather for hours. Tell the same stories over and over again, like about the year it rained so hard for two weeks straight or the time it didn't rain at all in July or about this storm or that one. And they love it. Farmers can talk about the weather for days and days and never get tired of it. It's a prime subject matter for them.

The other thing about farmers is how they look at the land. Come spring plowing they'll walk out and look over those fields before they start plowing and you see a kind of love in their eyes. Then there's the smell of spring plowing, that rich black dirt turning over. It's like a brand new start, a new beginning. Some people see farming as doing the same thing over and over, year in and year out, but farmers don't look at it that way at all. Every year is different. You get that land plowed early and hope you can get into the fields at the right time, when it ain't too wet, and plant them seeds and you never know what's gonna happen. Could be a good year and could be a not so good year but it's always an adventure.

A farmer will plow his land and then disk it—cut up the dirt some more—and then go out before he's planted in it and squat down with one leg tucked underneath him. He'll be balanced on the ball of one foot with the other leg setting out so his other foot is flat and from his knee to his shoe is straight. Then he'll reach down and pick up some dirt and let it run through his fingers or pick up a clod and crush it or maybe just hold the dirt in his hands and kinda shake it a bit like he's gonna throw some dice. He'll hunker down like that and look at that field a long time thinking about that land and that crop and wondering what he'll make, what kind of year it will be. He'll think about his family and what they need and things he'd like to buy for 'em. Then he'll think about what he needs and what he might be able to buy and what he knows he'll never get.

One time at Wendell's Store a bunch of farmers was sitting around the stove talking. They gather up there every Saturday night in the winter and talk about the crops and weather and other farming stuff. One night sitting around the wood stove they got to talking about things they'd like to have and each farmer got a little more extravagant than the last one. Like one would want a million dollars in his pocket in cold cash and another might want the million dollars and a mansion and another would want all that and a Cadillac too. Then it was Perry Hammerick's turn and he said, "I'd just like to have a smoothing harrow." Everybody looked at one another and just laughed, but then they all stopped talking like that cause Perry Hammerick told the truth for all of 'em. They all wanted something like a smoothing harrow, not too much to ask for but just out of reach. And mostly they all had to figure out how to get by and do without.

Seven

Mr. Bloodworth owns the land but we work it. We have a pretty good deal, better than some folks like us cause it's two thirds for us and one third for him. That means we get to keep two thirds of all the money we make off the crops but we have to pay for two thirds of things like seed and fertilizer. Course we have to pay it all a lot of times because Mr. Bloodworth might be laid up drunk when it comes time for spring planting or fixing a barn and we can't wait for him to sober up. That might take weeks or even months, usually a good solid month from the time he starts nipping until he's back sober again. Many's the time my Daddy's had to go get him out of some ditch or take him home when he's walking on the road blind stumbling drunk. Daddy hates that and it always makes him disgusted cause Mr. Bloodworth is a Big Shot in town. Has an important job with the county.

I come from a long line of sharecroppers. My Granddaddy Gregory, that would be my Daddy's daddy, sharecropped all his life and so did his Daddy. Further back than that I don't know but they'd all done pretty good and hadn't really moved around much. Landowners are glad to get good sharecroppers cause it keeps things steady. Especially white sharecroppers cause they're harder to find than the coloreds. The farm owners say that whites are more reliable and harder working. That's why my Great Grandaddy Gregory moved over from the next county, Hamilton, to St. John's County where we live now. We have lived in this county our whole lives. Granddaddy only worked on three farms his entire life and my Daddy has only worked on two. This farm is sixty acres and has some good land. Our cash crop is tobacco. We raise about eight acres of it.

Tell you the truth, Daddy is a man full of fears. He's scared of new people and new ideas as well as the powers that be. He's a man afraid to take chances and maybe that's why he's stayed a sharecropper. I love my Daddy but sometimes I don't really understand him for that but that's also part of being poor. People think being poor means not having any money in your pocket but that's not the whole case. It's a feeling of powerlessness and hopelessness and frustration that things will never get better cause the world has got you pinned down and won't let you up.

Having money is just part of it. Having opportunities and optimism and chances and respect is more important. Real poor people don't get any respect cause they don't respect themselves. It's like that Monopoly game where at the end if you don't have much money any little roll of the dice will wipe you out but if you've got plenty of money and own the right things a roll don't mean much. You can handle whatever comes your way.

Like most farmers, Daddy is a strong man. He can lift a hundred pound sack of feed and think nothing of it, just tote it around the barn. He's solid, too, not skinny or fat just solid. And Lord knows he sure is a worrier. Why, he can take an ounce of worry and roll it around for a spell and end up with twelve tons of disaster. I never knew nobody else who could take a grain of sand and worry it into a huge mountain boulder like Daddy.

Daddy has a right to worry about the crops and the weather and all that, I guess, but he worries if everything is going right, too. I'll ask him why he's worrying when everything is going right and he'll say he has to worry about what might be going to go wrong. Things might get too perfect so you ease up on your worrying and then whammo! So he always stays in practice. Me, I never worry about nothing. I figure you can't do nothing about most things anyway. It will rain when it rains and snow when it snows. Rest of the time you just play the hand dealt you and try to make do with what you got. I've never believed a problem was worth considering unless it was staring me full in the face.

Mama is kinda like me, not worrying about most stuff, but some of Daddy must've rubbed off on her cause the longer she lives the more she worries till I've noticed she's begun to fret over nothing. All the what if's and what would happen to you if it all happened when it isn't even happening. Them two will just sit around sometimes and make up things going wrong right outta thin air and then fret over them. It's like their hobby.

Mama is funny, always saying something witty or making some remark about somebody. Her whole side of the family is funny. Daddy and his side of the family take themselves real serious. The only time Daddy laughs is sometimes he'll crack a little joke to himself and chuckle but it really ain't funny to nobody else.

You can tell he's trying to be funny then. His whole side of the family is like that. Sometimes my uncles on the Gregory side will get to laughing and telling jokes when they get tanked up but mostly they get mean when they drink. There's that one little spot after a couple of beers when they get loose and funny and all that but they generally start out serious when they're sober and end up mean as hell when they're drunk. The Hevington side of the family gets funnier and funnier the drunker they get. Sometimes they'll pass out laughing and sleep with a big ole grin on their face.

Eight

I had to give up baseball this summer and that was hard for me to do. I love baseball and I'm good at it. Ever since I was nine years old I've been on the local team here. Twice a week I'd get home from school and go to practice and then once the season starts we'd play one night during the week and then once on Saturday afternoon.

I mostly played shortstop cause I could always catch just about anything, but I never was too good at hitting. One year I only got one important hit and that was a foul ball that somebody on the other team caught. There's a bunch of us boys who grew up together and we played ball together for years so nobody could hide anything from anybody else. You know, like everybody knows everbody else's weaknesses.

Back in Little League it was for kids aged nine to twelve and then Babe Ruth League was for kids aged thirteen to sixteen. That's a pretty big gap. Pretty much our whole team got thirteen years old at the same time and whammo we were in a league with older guys and one team had nothing but fifteen and sixteen year olds.

We lost every game that year, mostly by scores like 20-0 or something lopsided like that. It got so bad that our coaches decided we'd steal whenever we got on base. Or at least try to. Fact is we didn't get on base all that much so one day we're all at practice doing these sprints between bases and practicing slides and all that when Willie Glaser shows up late. Soon as he gets there Coach Morgan yells out, "Willie, can you steal?" Willie looks at him and says "I'll steal anything I can get my hands on." And he would, too.

But boy he had him an arm. Willie used to hunt squirrels for his family with rocks. He'd hit those squirrels in the head and knock 'em out, then pick 'em up and finish 'em off. Willie's daddy stayed drunk a lot but at the weekend stock car races over in the next county he drove a car he'd fixed up and that was a big deal. The Glaser's lived next door to my Uncle T-Bone and Aunt Tootie and their kids. One time when T-Bone, Tootie and the kids were away from the house Willie broke into their home to steal stuff but then the phone rang and Willie answered it and that's how he got caught.

Uncle T-Bone still hired Willie to cuss for him. Willie Glaser can cuss better than any other kid I ever knew. He has a way of coming up with new words and rearranging the old words to make 'em sound new. Willie Glaser makes cussing a fine art and his first cousin, Dougie Dunkett has the coolest way of smoking cigarettes I've ever seen. Has that cigarette just barely hanging on his lower lip so's it's hardly in his mouth. When Dougie talks that cigarette bounces up and down and when the smoke comes up into his face he'll close one eye and squint the other. Looks especially cool when he's playing cards.

It was in Dougie Dunkett's yard where I first saw an old tire cut up and half buried so those rubber triangles were sticking out at the top and flowers were planted in it. I thought that was the coolest thing I'd ever seen and I asked Daddy if we could get some tires for our yard. He said that's Mama's department so I asked her but she just said there was no way she'd do all that work just to make a flat tire look pretty.

The other cool thing about Dougie Dunkett's place is that he's got hub caps hanging up on the side of his house. That's a lot better than just a plain ole house any day. Sometimes he shoots his BB gun at them and you can hear that ping ping all over the place. I'm collecting hub caps too but so far I've only got one. Mama won't let me put it on the side of the house, said we already got a mirror inside. Daddy said lightning might hit it and burn the house down or somebody who needs a hub cap might steal it. He was worried especially about the colored.

Last year my Daddy took his plow down to Uncle T-Bone's in the spring to plow up T-Bone's garden. After he finished plowing Daddy left the plow down there for about a week. When he come back to get it the mould board was busted. Now it takes a lot to bust a mould board—that's the big steel part that curves up and turns the land over. The bottom of the plow is where the plow point goes that cuts through the ground.

Daddy just couldn't believe the mould board had been busted up like that. Willie Glaser and his two brothers, Ricky Joe and Phil Allen, were standing back a-ways just looking and Daddy knew who done it alright so he asked them, "Boys why did you bust up my plow?" But they all swore up and down they never busted that plow.

"No sir," they said. "We never busted that plow. Never touched that plow."

Well, Phil Allen was the youngest and a bit on the slow side. It took him a while to catch on to things but he was a real hard worker if you told him what to do and stayed on him. Phil Allen stayed around after Willie and Ricky Joe left so after awhile Daddy says, "Phil Allen, did you boys use a hatchet or hammer to bust up that plow?" And Phil Allen with those slow words of his says "Hatchet."

"Musta took awhile if you just had a hatchet," says Daddy.

"Yeah, we had to hit that thing a lot of times" said Phil Allen. Then he realized what he'd said and turned and took off running to his house.

Actually, I'd gotten pretty fed up with baseball, although I still loved it. There wasn't no rules that said everybody had to play at least two innings or anything like that so if the coach don't want you to play then you just sit on the bench game after game. That happened to some boys. Happened to me, too, a time or two, although I was always in the game when they needed somebody who could catch a ball. But I was getting behind in baseball. The other boys on the team didn't live on farms so they played all the time while I only got to practice twice a week. I throwed a lot of stones at trees and stuff but that's not the same.

There's three coaches for that team and they all coach so's their own sons can play. Their friend's sons, too. Everybody knows that. Since my Daddy ain't part of their crowd I was always shortchanged a bit but I was good enough to play shortstop cause I could out-catch 'em all, although one time the coaches kept me off the All Star team. They got to pick who they'd send and I should've gone. Everybody knew that but their kids went instead. That hurt bad and I've never forgotten it. Never will either. Something like that will never stop me from living my life. I figure I'll beat 'em at some other game somewhere down the line. I don't practice pay-back but pay-back comes to people who do things like that. You can always count on God to even things up eventually, so I leave things like that in His hands.

There's one coach, Tommy Senior Morgan, that has it in for me and I don't know why. I think he's just a jealous kind of person. I'm in the same class at school with his oldest son, Tommy Junior, and I always get better grades in school. Mr. Morgan don't like that and fusses at Tommy Junior. Says if anybody as stupid as me can get those grades then Tommy Junior ought to be able to get them, too. I'd hate to be the one to let Mr. Morgan know that Tommy Junior is one of the dumbest human beings on the face of this earth when it comes to school, but I reckon he'll wake up to that fact some day.

Two years ago I made the high school baseball and basketball teams and his son didn't but when it come to Little League or Babe Ruth baseball teams that Tommy Senior coached, I always got bumped for Tommy Junior.

Tommy Junior could be mean. One time he started giving other kids candy if they'd hate me and that worked a little while until the candy run out. Later, he told me his Daddy had given him the money for that. I never could figure out why his Daddy is like that, but he just is. It's hard to figure out the meanness in some folks. Mama said it comes from Adam and Eve so that line goes back a long way. I don't reckon it'll ever change now if'n it hasn't changed in all those millions of years since Adam and Eve got kicked out of their better homes and gardens. Daddy said it was Eve's fault for giving in to peer pressure from that snake and eating that apple.

Nine

I've got to say that I've learned some pretty valuable lessons from baseball. One time the coach finally let me pitch, although that was mostly reserved for the coach's sons. I almost pitched a no hitter but I walked a lot of guys and it was down to the last inning and the eighth batter was up. He was a little kid and I could tell he was scared by the look in his eyes when he got in the batter's box. I had me a good fast ball and that day it was even faster. I didn't want to walk this guy so I let up on my pitch and just threw it easy over the plate. Durned if he didn't poke out his bat on a half swing—he was left-handed—and punch that ball to left field. I've been mad at myself ever since. It's not that I mind losing a no-hitter. There's plenty of people in this world that ain't pitched a no hitter, so you can't be ashamed of that. It was the way I lost it that makes me mad. I lost it by not throwing my best pitch. That's a valuable lesson I learned: If you're gonna give up a no hitter, do it with your best pitch. Since then I've tried to give my best pitch every time in everything I've done. I still have regrets about that one pitch, though.

Another game I was playing shortstop and I was making all these incredible catches all over the place—backhanding hard hoppers and diving for balls to my left and throwing guys out and the crowd, what little there was (mostly parents of other kids and some assorted relatives) was really amazed. I was pretty full of myself and thought I was really amazing by making all those plays. Then a simple ground ball come straight at me. Nothing fancy, just ordinary and close to the ground and it went right through my legs. I must've taken my eyes off that ball or something. That taught me not to take nothing for granted or get too full of yourself.

Last year in the Babe Ruth League we had the hottest team around. We didn't lose a single game all season. Nobody around thought we could be beat and we thought the same thing. In the championship game we played a team we'd beaten twice that season and they almost didn't want to show up. Neither did we cause we thought we was too good for all that. Well, buddy, let me tell you that we never really got things together that game and next thing you know it was 4-2 their favor and we couldn't get any hits and they started believing they could win. It was like a big tide turned against us and there wasn't nothing we could do about it. We always thought we could turn it on or turn it off whenever we felt like it but we sure couldn't do it in that game. We'd already been talking and acting like champions so at the end of that game our heads was hanging low and we didn't want to talk to nobody or see nobody or nothing. Showed me that nobody's too big to get beat.

Oh, I almost forget to tell about that one important hit I got that first year in Babe Ruth League. See, the bases were loaded and I was up and there was only one out and the pitcher was good. Like I said before, I wasn't all that great at hitting but I swung at a pitch and hit it pretty good, a long foul ball down the left field line. Well, I knew that if that left fielder caught the ball the guy on third would tag up and head for home but if he dropped that ball or just let it go there wasn't much chance of me hitting it like that again. Well, the left-fielder caught it and the guy on third tagged up and scored and that was the only run we scored that game. Lost 23-1.

My best memory in baseball came during my last year in Little League. I was playing center field and we was at Lynnville. It was the bottom of the last inning, two out, two on, score tied and Frankie Thompson was up to bat. There was a man on first and second and if one of 'em scored we'd lose the game. Well Frankie got aholt of that ball and gave it a ride like you wouldn't believe. It was to my left and way over my head but I'd studied the baseball card that week of Willie Mays making his famous catch of Vic Wertz's fly ball so I pretended I was Willie Mays and just took off running after that ball. I wasn't sure I could even get there but I kept running as hard as I could and running and running and the ball was finally pretty close to me so I just reached up like Willie Mays and be danged if I didn't catch that ball!

Well, our team went crazy and we ended up winning that game in extra innings. My Daddy never went to my baseball games cause he always had farm work to do but a couple of nights later at dinner he looked at me and asked "What kind of catch did you make the other day?"

I looked at him kinda funny cause he never wanted to know about my games, but then I said "Well, I had to run a long ways to get it" and he said that one of my coaches, Melvin Davidson, was down at the River View Tavern the night after the game and all he could talk about was that catch I'd made. Daddy said that all night long Coach Davidson drank and talked about that catch.

That made me feel pretty good but also a little disappointed. See, word was out in that game that a Major League scout was in the stands. Looking back on it all it was probably true but the guy probably came to watch his nephew or something like that. Anyway, I kept expecting that scout to show up at my house and sign me up for the Major Leagues or at least talk to me some. I didn't realize until later that Major League scouts generally don't sign up twelve-year olds after just one catch, no matter how good it was.

In April this year the team had three games and I played in them all. But for the fourth game I was dressed in my uniform and ready to go when Daddy stopped me. "Son, I need you to plow," he said.

It was spring planting and there was a lot to be done. He just kept looking at me and I kept looking down. Then I just went out and got on that tractor in my baseball uniform and started plowing. I was mad at first but then I just kept plowing and started thinking about other things. And that was the end of baseball.

Ten

Soon as I got in high school I signed up for the school band, but Mama and Daddy didn't want me to have music lessons so I had to drop band after I'd signed up for it. They said you had to have music in you if you was going to play music and nobody in our family had music in them. Since none of my relatives was musical I had to agree with them, but I wanted to play music in the worst kind of way so I saved up my money until I had $15 and sent away to Sears and Roebuck for a Silvertone guitar. It was small and had a sunburst finish and it was beautiful. I learned how to tune it and started learning to play. I realized pretty quick that I needed a good book so I ordered a Mel Bay book from Montgomery Ward for $2.98 and when that came I set about learning chords. Until that book got to my mailbox I just plunked out tunes.

Anybody with any sense at all can tell you that in order to play a guitar you need callouses on your fretting fingers. I didn't have no callouses and the only way to get callouses is to just keep playing. That means your fingers get puffy and blistered and so sore you can't hardly touch nothing and then they break and bleed but if you really want to learn to play the guitar, and the Good Lord knows I sure did, then you just keep on practicing.

Practicing at something you're not good at is hard. It wasn't like school work; nobody made me do it. I'd get so frustrated I'd just want to throw that guitar away or smash it to pieces, but I'd put it down a while, walk around and then pick it up again. First time I tried to play a chord it sounded dreadful. I killed the strings so everywhere I had my fingers there was this dead thud sound when I strummed, but then I got to the point where I could play a chord all right but I couldn't change to another chord, so that took a long time, strumming along on one chord and then changing to another.

I made quite a racket when I first started practicing and nobody wanted to hear me. Daddy kept saying I was wasting my time and it wouldn't amount to nothing no how. Besides, it just kept me from doing something worthwhile. That's exactly what he said. He said "You're wasting your time cause this ain't gonna amount to nothin' and it keeps you from doing something worthwhile." So I couldn't practice during daylight on a working day. At night nobody wanted me anywhere near them so the only place for me to practice was in the bathroom with the door closed.

Every night I'd go into that bathroom and shut the door and sit on the throne with the Mel Bay book spread out on the clothes hamper in front of me and practice those chords. Daddy and them mostly watched TV. During the commercials, whenever anybody wanted to go to the bathroom, they'd bang on the door and I'd have to clear out and then, as soon as they finished their business, I'd go back in again. They'd fuss a little at me, but not much cause they was mostly involved in the TV shows so I had the bathroom to myself most of every night.

It was a lot better on Sunday afternoons. I'd go over to the barn then to practice, although Daddy used to say he was worried about the hogs getting sick and that the milk cows might dry up from my singing and playing. Course Sundays after church and dinner was always visiting day and people might come by or we might all load up in our car and show up at somebody else's house to visit. That's what Sunday was all about.

Being 16 years old I'd lost a lot of desire for visiting relatives, especially since I was caught between being a kid and a grown up and neither side felt too comfortable, so I'd stay home whenever I could. If people showed up I'd just say my howdy's and then amble off to the barns. It seemed like a nice compromise and to tell you the truth, the grown-ups was probably relieved I was in the barn a-plunking on my guitar anyway. That way they only had to ask me if I knew any tunes right after they got there and listen to me play just one. Daddy drilled into me real good that nobody really wanted to hear me play. That's exactly what he said. He said, "Nobody really wants to hear you play." Then he said they was just being polite when they asked so I was supposed to play something quick and then stop and then they didn't have to deal with me wanting to hang around grown-ups talking grown up talk.

By the summer of 1965 I'd gotten pretty good on the guitar. I could play and sing all the hot new stuff like "I've Got a Tiger By The Tail" by Buck Owens and "England Swings" by Roger Miller, "Girl on the Billboard" by Del Reeves, "Saginaw, Michigan" by Lefty Frizzell and "Understand Your Man" by Johnny Cash. My favorites were Buck Owens, Johnny Cash, Bill Anderson and George Jones but my all time favorite was Roger Miller. Lord I bought every Roger Miller album I could and learned every single song on those albums. I could play his big hits like "Chug-a-Lug" and "Dang Me," although I never could quite get his guitar runs exactly right. I even knew his album stuff like "Squares Make the World Go Round," "Got 2 Again" and "There I Go Dreaming Again." Boy, I sure loved Roger Miller.

Eleven

Soon after the school Talent Show I run into Billy Boy Lindsley and we started talking about guitars. I knew Billy Boy cause he was on my baseball team. He was two years older than me but only a year ahead of me in school, so he graduated right after the Talent Show.

Billy Boy asked me if I'd like to come over to his house sometime and bring my guitar. He said he'd got a guitar last Christmas and he'd learned a few chords and would like to try to play them with somebody else. Asked if I'd like to be a guinea pig. Naturally I agreed and then I asked Mama and Daddy about it. Mama said she couldn't see no sense in going over to somebody's house and disturbing their peace and that the Lindsley's could live without my racket. She said I had better things to do and didn't want me to go but I kept begging her to let me so finally she said to Daddy, "Catnap, what do you think of Compton going over to the Lindsley's house." Daddy just sat there quiet for awhile and then said, "Roadkill said Perry Hammerick was going to plant tobacco in that field down past the Lindsley's." So the very next day I went over to Billy Boy's house.

I got to the Lindsley's house right after supper and Billy Boy was sitting in his living room just holding his guitar like he was gonna play but his whole family was watching TV. He had a younger brother, Bobby Boy, and a sister, Glenda. I thought that was nice of his family to let him sit in the living room with his guitar cause Daddy never would let me do that. Said I had to go play somewhere's else if I had my guitar with me cause nobody wanted to hear that racket and besides everybody would rather watch TV and if they wanted to hear music they could turn on the radio.

The Lindsley's only lived about two miles from us, just past Wendell's store on the way down to the River View Tavern. Mr. Lindsley, whose real name was Eugene, worked for the J. Benjamin O'Connell Electric Company as an electrician. J. Benjamin was known as Shock O'Connell. The Lindsley's house was a small, box-shaped house, white wooden with green shutters, that felt small but real cozy.

Well, I walked into Billy Boy's house and said "howdy" to everybody and then Billy Boy got up and said "Let's go into the bedroom" so we did and I took out my guitar and sat on the edge of one of the single beds. Billy Boy sat on the other one so we were facing each other.

"What songs can you play?" he asked me and I told him I could play just about anything on the radio. He said he'd learned "Camptown Races" and "Frauline," which were both old songs. I said I didn't care so we played "Frauline" and Billy Boy sang and I picked up some harmony on the chorus. Actually, I mostly just sang the melody with him on the chorus cause I really didn't know much about harmony at that time but I soon slid into harmony singing, even though I didn't know what to call it at first. It started a little bit when Billy Boy sang "Camptown Races." Then it was my turn and I sang "Send Me the Pillow That You Dream On," the old Hank Locklin song. Billy Boy knew the words to that song too, so he started singing it with me, but his voice took the melody and mine just moved into a harmony part. That knocked us both out so we sang that song again.

Then we played some more songs. I played along with whatever Billy Boy sang and even added some lead runs and a break in some songs but Billy Boy couldn't quite play along with me. Billy Boy only knew what Billy Boy knew on the guitar and that was about it so I ended up doing most of the playing but boy our voices fit together, especially on Everly Brothers songs like "Let It Be Me" and "Bye, Bye Love" or on Louvin Brothers songs like "When I Stop Dreaming" and "I Take the Chance" and "Must You Throw Dirt in My Face." Both of us was surprised the other one knew that last song.

I was surprised to find that Billy Boy loved country music like I did. He'd bought a bunch of albums and listened to country music on the radio. Mr. Lindsley owned some country records too, which is how we found out about the Delmore Brothers, who did "Blues Stay Away From Me." We learned that song the first night after Billy Boy played me that record.

I had gotten so's I could play anything I heard on the radio or on a record if it was a country song so I could play pretty near anything I heard Billy Boy play that night, especially if I'd heard it somewheres else before. Billy Boy didn't know as many songs on the guitar as I did, and couldn't pick up the chords as fast, so he mostly sang while I played and sang harmony. It got so that I felt like I was transported into another world every time Billy Boy and I locked into a song we both knew and where I could do a harmony part to his lead vocal. Sometimes we'd be singing a ballad and it'd feel like we was just floating along on a cloud. It sounded pretty, too. Mrs. Lindsley came in and told us so.

We did a bunch of songs that night. We did "Oh, Susannah" cause Billy Boy had just learned that out of a guitar book, some old Eddy Arnold songs like "Anytime," "I Really Don't Want to Know," "Bouquet of Roses," "Molly, Darling," and "You Don't Know Me." Billy Boy knew a lot of Eddy Arnold songs cause his Daddy had a lot of Eddy Arnold records. The Lindsley's didn't like Roger Miller as much as I did, but I sang "Chug-a-Lug," "King of the Road," "Invitation to the Blues," and "Billy Bayou," which were all Roger Miller songs, that night. By the end of the night I felt like I'd drank from a fountain of living water and my soul was refreshed. Singing with Billy Boy was almost a spiritual experience and as soon as the clock hit nine and his Mama said we needed to quit we started making plans to get together again.

I spent most Saturday nights over at Billy Boy's house that summer. Billy Boy had gotten a job with Shock O'Connell right after he graduated from high school so that's how he could afford to buy a car. Every Saturday night he'd come by and pick me up and take me back over to his house so's we could play.

We talked about starting a band but nothing ever came of it. Daddy and Mama both said it was all foolishness whenever I brought up the idea of playing in a band, said I ought not go out in public and embarrass the whole family. That's exactly what they said: "If you go play and sing out in public you'll embarrass the whole family." They said that playing and singing around the house was bad enough. I always closed my eyes when I sang and Mama said it was a good thing I did that cause then I couldn't see other people suffering. She said if I ever sang with my eyes open I'd quit in the middle of the first song and never play anything ever again. I figured there might be some wisdom in that so I kept my eyes closed, but every now and then I'd sneak a peak. I only played for relatives and I never saw any of them get sick but after I'd finished my song they never asked me to play another one. Once I asked Mama if maybe I should do two or three songs next time some relatives came over but Mama said "no." Said the reason why people preferred to listen to the radio was cause you could always turn it off. She said if I played a bunch of songs I'd just be a radio without a knob. That's exactly what she said: "You'll just be a radio without a knob."

    I wanted them to come over to the Lindsley's to hear me and Billy Boy sing together but they wouldn't never do that. I told them how good me and Billy Boy's voices blended and how many songs we knew but Mama always said, "It's bad enough having to listen to one hound dog howl. I don't want to have to listen to two." Everytime I asked Daddy about coming over to the Lindsley's to hear me and Billy Boy sing he'd start talking about the crops or something with the farm.

    Boy did I thoroughly love the radio. For some reason I didn't care much for the TV. There were some shows I liked such as the country music shows and all but mostly I practiced my guitar or listened to the radio. Daddy and them couldn't get enough of that TV set. Next to being over at the Lindsley's house and singing with Billy Boy, the best thing in my life was sitting in my room at night listening to the radio. I loved finding country music stations all across the country.

    I really got a kick out of finding different cities at night on the radio. I'd listen to a station from Buffalo, New York or Boston or Cleveland or Cincinnati or somewheres else and it felt like I was traveling. And Lord, I wanted to travel, wanted to get out and see the world, wanted to go to all kinds of different places and hobnob with all kinds of different people. Course I was stuck on that old farm and nobody was buying me a ticket for anywhere but listening to that radio I could travel some. Most every night I'd try to find some station in a different city and hear what was going on. I mention all this to show why giving up baseball wasn't as hard as it would've been a couple of years before. Baseball got to be less important the more I got into music, plus I could practice the guitar and learn songs by myself but I needed a whole team to practice baseball.

    In addition to music becoming more important in my life, there was also another reason why baseball was less important beginning in the late spring of 1965.

Twelve

Don't ask me to explain this cause I can't. It just snuck up on me one day and seized me, I reckon. One day in May before the end of school I was just my normal regular self and then I sorta woke up into a new world and found myself staring at Kathleen Holt. I started thinking about her every single minute of the day. I couldn't think of nothing by itself no more because no matter what I was doing or thinking she was perched there too. It was like a split screen TV. You know how there's a big picture and then a little picture in the corner? Well, that's the way it was with Kathleen. If she wasn't the big picture she was always the little picture in the corner and the only way to get rid of that little picture was if she was the big picture.

Kathleen Holt was not the most beautiful girl in school but she was probably second. The prettiest was Patty Sherman and I'd had a crush on her going back to elementary school. I remember back in the third grade I thought I could marry Patty Sherman right then and there and just get over all the worry about finding a wife and be done with it. I knew I'd be happy with that decision for the rest of my life, not that I was thinking about getting a wife or anything back in the third grade. That kinda stuff never really worried me but Aunt Tootie and Aunt Noodles was always talking about so and so not having a girlfriend or boyfriend and wondering when they would or that so and so was starting to make eyes at somebody or other and wondering what would come of it all and what the kids would look like and other nonsense like that. They worried a lot over single people and wanted everybody fixed up and married so they could talk about two people instead of one. I guess I didn't want them to be talking about me like that, so a quick marriage seemed best.

The best I can recollect is that I was in the school cafeteria eating when I found myself totally engrossed in Kathleen. In fact, I was staring at her. She kinda glanced at me and looked back down at her food but I kept staring and I couldn't stop. After lunch I kept thinking about her and by the time I got into bed that night she was all I could think about. I'd imagine us doing stuff together like taking walks and me picking her flowers or drinking soda pops and talking or her sitting and watching me play ball or listening to me play the guitar and sing or maybe listening to a Roger Miller album together. I remember Dougie Dunkett saying that the perfect date was a girl helping you wax your car under a shade tree on a Sunday afternoon so I tried to imagine us waxing a car together too.

Trying to imagine washing a car with Kathleen was real hard to do. Mama said I was the only boy she ever knew that didn't like to polish and shine on a car in my spare time. On Sundays they'd send me over to the barns to wash the car and I'd drive it over, but then I'd take out my guitar and play some songs or listen to the radio. Finally, when I figured I needed to be gettin' back—or when I heard them yellin' for me—I'd turn on the hose and get that car real good and wet and then I'd jump in and drive it back to the house. Well, the dust from that gravel road would always settle on that wet car and then Mama'd fuss at me. She said I was the only person who could make a car dirtier by washing it.

There were several rather severe problems with my relationship with Kathleen Holt from its very inception. First, Kathleen was an older woman, being born in February while I was born at the end of October. That makes a big difference with young women who generally want to be with older men. Two years older is ideal, I think, because I noticed the girls in the tenth grade went out with seniors and the ideal beau for girls in the eleventh grade was somebody in his first year of college. Oh how those high school juniors and seniors would swoon over a college boy. If some high school girl was going out with a college boy who only came back on the weekends, well you might say she was at the peak on the social scale.

Actually, avoiding younger men is not a lifelong obsession with women. It may be for high school girls, as far as I can tell, cause they don't want to be caught dead with anybody younger. Same with college girls from what I hear but older women ain't nearly as picky. I know for a fact that Leola Lippitt was 44 years old when she up and married a man ten years younger without batting an eyelash. If she had batted an eyelash he would certainly have felt it cause Leola always wore eyelashes that looked like brooms. That's what Aunt Noodles and Aunt Tootie always said when they talked about Leola. I heard Aunt Tootie say once "You know Leola, with those brooms on her eyes, has swept many a room looking for a man."

Aunt Noodles and Aunt Tootie also said that younger man was Leola's fourth husband and all except the first one had been younger than her. The second and third were only a couple years younger but this one spanned a decade. Leola lived across the road from my Aunt Tootie so that supplied our family with plenty of material during get-togethers. Leola liked to swish when she walked and I heard Mama say one time that Leola couldn't walk through a double door without bruising both hips and just before she got married this last time Aunt Tootie said about Leola that "it was ashamed to have such a big swing and no porch to put it on." Right after the marriage I heard Aunt Noodles tell Mama she'd "better watch Compton if Leola shakes loose again cause next time she's liable to be robbing cradles." I don't think I was supposed to hear that but I resented being called a baby when I was 16 years old. Also, I always thought Leola was a lady with a lot of class because she had a cement bird bath and two pink flamingos in her front yard. That, to me, was a cut above the ordinary.

Kathleen Holt lived in downtown Lynnville and her father worked at the bank. In fact, he was president of the bank, so I guess that means he didn't work at all, just sat around being president and raking in the money. I'd seen her house and it was a two story brick job with shutters painted green. I don't know why she had shutters on her house because it looked like they never closed them. None of my relatives had shutters cause we had screens on our windows and Daddy always said it was a big improvement on a house to have screens instead of shutters to keep out flies. Besides, shutters made a house so dark. Aunt Tootie and Aunt Noodles both had awnings over their front windows because they said it gave shade but you could still see out. The Holt's house had some big trees in the front yard so they probably didn't need the shade. Most of my aunts just had mimosa trees for shade in their yard.

After I fell in love with Kathleen Holt I couldn't take my eyes off her or stop thinking about her but I never said anything to her. I wanted to but I just couldn't think of nothing to say. I tried and I tried. I did find out that she liked the Beatles and so I liked them right away, too. Actually, I liked them all along ever since I saw them on The Ed Sullivan Show, although at first I said I couldn't stand 'em cause of their hair and because they were foreigners, which was the judgment all my relatives passed on them. But when I found out Kathleen Holt liked 'em I went right out and bought a Beatles album. That was hard for me to do because I saved my money careful to buy country music albums but this was important to Kathleen and, besides, it was a good album too.

I set about learning some of the Beatles songs but I never could quite get any of them right or even close like I could with Buck Owens or Roger Miller. I tried to sing "I Want To Hold Your Hand" but Charlene said it sounded like a coon dog trying to do opera. Then I tried to learn "I Saw Her Standing There" but Charlene laughed at me and said I got the words wrong. I sang "She was just seventeen and you know what I mean and the way she looked was way beyond repair." Well Charlene said the word wasn't "repair" but actually "compare." I kept working on those Beatle songs, although some of them seemed impossible for me to learn. They had a lot of minor chords and weird keys and I was pretty much a straight ahead three chord country guitar player and country music was the stuff I loved. Still, for Kathleen I kept trying to learn Beatles songs.

With school letting out soon and all and me not knowing whether I'd see Kathleen during the whole summer and not knowing whether I could actually stand not having her around to stare at, I decided I would call her up and ask her for a date. I'd never asked a girl for a date before. In fact, I'd never even thought about going on a date before so I had to figure out how to do it and not let my folks know cause I knew they'd tease me and joke about it and tell me to stay away from her.

Kathleen Holt was just way beyond my reach and I knew that but I have always felt that true love will fill in any deep ditch of differences that might separate people. I started working up my courage to call her during May and practiced dialing her number with the phone still on the hook, then I went to the phone booth right outside Wendell's Store and stood inside that phone booth six times, nervous as a long-tailed cat in a room full of rocking chairs, before I lost my nerve and got out. Finally, the seventh time was the night before the last day of school and I thought it would be nice to get a date and then see her again the next day so I dropped a dime in the phone and dialed her number and her father answered.

"Can I speak to Kathleen?" I asked. He said "Surely," and then I heard him calling for her and she came to the phone and said, "Hello?"
"Hello, Kathleen?" I said.
"Yes?" she said.
"This is Compton Gregory."
There was a pause and then she said "Oh, hi."
"Would you like to go out Saturday night?" I said.
She paused again. "No, I've got other plans."
"O.K." I said. "Good bye." Then I hung up. I was shaking like a leaf on a windy day. Felt like a cold sweat was coming on, too.

The next day I avoided her and couldn't even look at her. After going through all that, I felt embarrassed to be near her but I was still madly in love with her.

Thirteen

It took us over a year to get the roof fixed on our house because of Mr. Bloodworth being drunk and then not having the money and whatnot but finally, a week after school was out, it got fixed when Mr. Bloodworth had some tarpaper and sheetrock delivered. He didn't tell us it was coming or nothing. One day a truck from the lumber company just showed up and dropped it off. Me and Daddy and Uncle T-Bone dropped everything else and got to work right away. Two days later it was done.

There had always been a leak or two somewheres in the ceiling ever since I can remember but a year ago last March it started leaking bad during the spring storms. After that, every time it rained me and Daddy would walk around the house looking at the ceiling and when we'd see sheetrock sagging we'd get up quick and drive a nail in to let the water through. There got to be so many holes in the ceiling that every time it rained Mama couldn't cook cause all the pots and pans were used to catch water. We even bought two of them little plastic blow up swimming pools for when it rained so's we could catch water. We always put one swimming pool in the middle of the living room and the other pool in a corner of the living room, which meant there was just enough space in the living room to walk between them.

Storms were real hard cause you had to unplug everything and get the TV antenna wire outside the house. Lighting can strike a house out in the country easy and blow up everything. Finally, it got so that when it rained down hard it just poured right on through that roof. The part I hated the most was walking around at 3 or 4 in the morning cause you was tired and sleepy and everybody else was asleep but you had to stay awake cause the whole ceiling could come crashing in. That only happened once, in the middle room of the house, but boy was it a mess I reckon. Big ole hole you could look up and see the two by fours. Good thing we didn't have no big diamond chandelier hanging there like rich folks do cause it sure would've busted.

Daddy he did his best to remind Mr. Bloodworth about the roof but Mr. Bloodworth had other fish to fry. That's what Daddy always said when he come back from talking with Mr. Bloodworth. He'd say, "He's got other fish to fry besides our roof."

Our house was what folks call a "shotgun" house cause, as the saying goes, you could stand at one end and shoot a gun all the way to the back of the house. Actually, it was a step above the shotgun houses the coloreds lived in because it was wider, which meant there were two rooms down the house instead of just a real narrow house with one room leading to the next.

There was a porch out front that we got screened in. It was little—about eight feet square—but room enough for some chairs to sit on in the summer. The first room was the living room and off to the side of that was Daddy and Mama's bedroom. Originally I think it had just been a square house with those two rooms. The next room was what we called the middle room and just off that room, which was the longest, was the kitchen and then the bathroom. The bathroom was just another room until Daddy put the toilet in when I was in the fourth grade and then we added a tub when I was in the sixth grade. Before that there was an outhouse down back of the house about fifty yards away. You walked out the side door of our house, past the wood pile and then down a little gully and there it was. You always want an outhouse on the side of a hill if you can get it and that's how ours was, but the outhouse blowed over in a big storm the year after the indoor toilet was put in.

Before Daddy put the indoor bathroom in we had to use pots at night or in bad weather. We kept them pots under the beds. Mostly Mama and Charlene used the pots, then me and Daddy had to empty them the next day. Daddy always went outside to do his business. I usually just went out on the side step unless I had to do number two, then it was all the way down to that outhouse until it blowed over.

The two back rooms were bedrooms. The first was for Charlene and the very last one was for me. Those last two rooms were really just one room divided in two. My room was the smallest and you had to walk through Charlene's room to get to it. There wasn't no door on the doorway, just a curtain, and when Daddy bought a freezer to store meat in it was kept in my room, which meant that after the freezer was put in my bedroom along one wall, there was just enough room for a single bed, a dresser and one of those put together closets we got from Sears. Mama's and Daddy's bedroom had their double bed, a dresser and one of those old cedar chests. Boy was it great to lift that cedar chest top up and take a big whiff. Mama kept special stuff in there that she called her hair looms. Clothes were kept in cardboard boxes with lots of moth balls and they always had that thick musky smell when you took out the winter clothes after summer or the summer clothes after winter. There was also a fold out bed—we always called it a roll-a-way bed—in their bedroom that Charlene and I slept in when we was young. That bed folded straight up—each end pulled up and locked together on top—and it was great fun to crawl in that folded up bed.

For a long time I couldn't sleep in my own room in the winter cause it was so cold but one winter I just made up my mind to do it and I did. There was no heat back there. There were two wood stoves in the house but they was in the living room and middle room and they went out at night. The house was set up on cinder blocks and the wind just got under the floor at night and made those floors so icy cold that on a winter morning you'd get up and when your feet hit the floor you'd get a headache. The windows always leaked and when it snowed at night there'd always be a pile of snow on the inside window sill in the morning. When it rained we used a lot of rags and towels on the windows and the frost would always be on the inside of the window as well as the outside. On cold mornings I'd wake up and stick my head out of those covers and I could see my breath and that's how I could tell how cold it was. I hated to get out of that warm bed so bad on those icy cold mornings but then I'd have to go to the bathroom so bad I couldn't stay in, so I'd stay there until I couldn't hold it no longer and then make a run for it.

Daddy usually made the fire in the stove in the morning when he got up but as I got older I had to do it now and then. Well, you've got to keep an eye on a fire to make sure it gets going good. One cold morning I fixed a fire real quick, then jumped back in bed and the fire went out. Well, I'll tell you that whole family was mad at me cause when they got up the house was still freezing cold and I'd been laying in bed.

On those cold winter nights I'd sleep in long underwear, then flannel pajamas over that and then a pair of socks. When I got in the bed I'd lay there and Mama would pull covers over me until there were so many covers and they were so heavy that once I got in I couldn't roll over so I had to figure out how I wanted to lay before the covers went on. Not much tossing and turning but then I've always been one of those people who just gets in a bed, lays down and goes to sleep. Actually, during this past winter, which was extra cold it seemed like, I got an electric pad for Christmas which went on my bed. I'd turn that on at night and sleep on it and it kept me warm.

In the summer it was real hot in that back bedroom. We only had one big fan for the whole house, which we kept in the living room, so if I tried to stay in my room I'd just sweat, although it was alright for sleeping cause it always cooled off at night. On hot summer nights my folks would put that big electric fan in my bedroom by the window and let it blow through the whole house. Well, don't you know that one time I took off my old shoes that were dirty and sweaty and God-awful smelly and didn't think once about all that when I dropped them down right in front of that fan before I crawled in bed. That fan blew that smell through the house all night long. Boy was Daddy and Mama mad the next morning when they got up and the house stunk to high heaven. They let me know about it, too. I was a lot more careful about dropping my shoes off after that and I think Daddy and Mama always checked on me, too.

I stunk the house up real bad another time just this past spring. That was when I had to clean out the barn at the beginning of April. All during the winter we just keep throwing more and more straw where the cows and hogs bed down so every spring there's about two feet of that straw all smelly wet and packed together. Well, Daddy had gone off somewhere Saturday morning and I had to clean out that whole barn. It was hard work but I stuck to it. I'd load up that manure spreader and then hook it to the tractor and take it out and spread the manure on a field. I'd drive up and down the field while the blades on the spreader scattered the natural fertilizer.

There was a couple of fields that needed manure and one of them was right in front of our house. I covered that field pretty good but when I come to the house for dinner at noon—that's when Daddy got home—he and Mama were having a fit. Seems there was a real strong breeze that day blowing over that field towards the house and Mama was doing her spring cleaning and all the windows was wide open. That made our whole house stink like cow and pig manure. I'd never thought about the wind blowing until then.

*F*ourteen

Four years ago we had real good crops and Mama got a wool rug for the living room. We'd put that rug down in the winter and then roll it up in the summer and keep it on the side of the wall. The rest of the house had linoleum rugs. Rolling up that wool rug was men's work and me and Daddy had to roll it up, then take it outside and hang it up and beat it until it was clean but Mama was particular about how you beat that rug. I used to like to get a baseball bat and pretend I was hitting home runs but she didn't care for that method at all. She liked me to use the flat side of the broom and wanted me to swing at pitches all over the place—high, low, inside and outside.

The same year we got the wool rug we got a couch that came in three pieces so you could move it around. It was one of those couches that fit in a corner—the middle section was curved—so that's where it sat, in our living room corner. Right behind it on the wall was a great big piece of particle board that Mama pasted a picture on each side of. On one side was this snowy scene of a mountain and on the other side was a green scene of the same mountain. Real big picture—about four foot by six foot—and it pretty much covered almost the whole wall. Every summer we had up the summer scene, then we'd have to flip it over in the winter for that snow scene.

There were two other pictures I remember in our house. In the living room was a big picture of a clipper ship sailing on the water—full of sails—and in the middle room was a picture of three deer, a doe and two fawns and the doe was looking right at the camera. They were both photographs. One year we got another picture which was on sale at the Five and Dime. It was of a stream running through a valley between mountains and in the corner was an artist's name. One day in school we had to do a report on an artist and a bunch of kids already had Norman Rockwell so I had to come up with an artist's name and I'd never heard of none of them so I looked at the corner of that painting and decided to do a report on the name written there, but I couldn't find a single thing on him anywhere. At first the teacher was pretty excited when I told her this name. She thought I musta known something about art, I guess, cause I knew this name she'd never heard of but then she must've caught on. That let me know we was having to write some report about a subject that she didn't know too much about herself.

The year we got the couch we also got a chair that matched, which meant we put our old couch and chair outside. We was going to give them to a colored family, and we did later, but they sat outside our house for a little while. During that time a hard heavy rain came. Well, I'd just gotten a yellow rain coat with one of them hats that lets you peak out and a new pair of galoshes so I decided to go outside in that rain get-up and sit in that old stuffed chair. Sat there a long time. Found out the rain coat worked pretty good, but I still got wet.

When I come back in the house Mama 'bout to had a caniption. Didn't know I'd been outside and wondered what fool would do such a thing as set out in a hard driving rain on purpose. Mama's biggest criticism against people was that they didn't have sense enough to come in out of the rain. That's exactly what she'd say about some fool, "He don't have sense enough to come in out of the rain." You always knew if she said that about somebody, she didn't think too highly of them and here she had to face her own flesh and blood in that sorry state. She did not hesitate to inform me that I was filled with stupidity and dumbness. It must have galled her to come to grips with the fact that she'd given birth to a creature who didn't have sense enough to come in out of the rain.

Actually I enjoyed the whole experience. What's the sense of owning a good rain coat if you can't use it except for accidents and disasters? And shouldn't you test something out real good before you need to use it?

Rain was something we didn't have to worry ourselves too much about in the summer of 1965. We finally got the roof fixed so it didn't leak like crazy and then it didn't rain so we couldn't find out if we'd covered everything or not. Wasn't really no need to fix the roof that summer although, like the old story goes, the guy didn't fix the roof when it wasn't raining cause it didn't leak and when it was raining he couldn't do it cause it was too wet, but I think we played it smart to fix our roof when we did.

We did have some rain in the spring and couldn't get into the fields to plant as early as we wanted to and then when we finally got all the seed in the ground it didn't rain at all. A few sprinkles in May but by June it was bone dry and there wasn't a rain cloud to be seen anywhere. Daddy worried more every day and sometimes I'd see him just sitting at the kitchen table and staring at nothing. The summer before it had been dry too and we hadn't had much of a crop. We'd sold our previous year's crop of tobacco in April and it wasn't much but we could probably make it one more year if we had a good crop to let us catch up but two dry years in a row was murder. I remember Daddy saying it always rained ten minutes before it was too late. Well, too late came last year and this year it still wasn't raining. I didn't know how we was going to make it but I never talked to Daddy about it. He never brought the subject up either but stayed quiet a lot. I knew he was thinking about it heavy, though.

Fifteen

The first week after I got out of school in June I spent walking up and down tobacco rows with a hoe digging out weeds between the plants. Now that's a hard job cause you just have to walk all day long and that hoe will give you blisters if there's much grass. Crops don't grow in dry weather but weeds do. In fact, weeds grow better in bad weather so I spent that week in the tobacco fields and then had to go into the corn and soy bean fields. After a couple of days to fix the roof I started cultivating with the tractors and at the end of June we got in our winter wheat.

Actually, hoeing weeds and cultivating crops ain't all that boring to me cause I use the time to write songs. I'll start on an idea when I'm hoeing, maybe just a line that I'll sing over and over until another line comes to me to follow it. Sometimes I'll just get a melody I'll hum over and over until some words come along with it and then sometimes I'll wake up with a title in my head, or I'll hear somebody else talking and they'll say something that I think will make a good line or title or will fit into a song somehow. I'll roll those words over in my mind till they work themselves into a song. Sometimes I'll work on a song all day long before I get it done and then after work as soon as I get back to the house, even before I have supper, I'll pick up my guitar and work out the chords and stuff. I'll write it down too, so's I won't forget it.

One day I come up with the title "Greenback Romeo" out in the fields and I wrote that whole song in my head and had to remember it until I got back to the house and wrote it down. It went like this:

Women make hot love to cold, cold cash
Something that a poor boy just don't have
I'm alone wherever I go
Cause I'm not a Greenback Romeo

Women are happy and never mean
If the love that you bring is green
But love runs out when the cash runs low
Then you're not a Greenback Romeo

Instead of a regular chorus, I had a bridge in the middle. It went like this:

You can tell a rich man young or old
By the clothes he wears and the girls he holds
And in a big crowd you can pick a rich man
By the good lookin' girl a-holdin' his hand

My final verse was:

Women will treat you like a king
If it's money that you bring
But love runs out when the cash runs low
Then you're not a Greenback Romeo

One morning I just had a melody and I kept running it over and over in my head until some words fell into it. Here are those words:

Just got a letter that started Dear John
I found someone else, now you're all alone
She wished me success but it will never fail
It's a broken heart from the U.S. Mail
Open up an envelope expectin' quite a thrill
But lookin' back at me is an unpaid bill
I always look for good things but never seen it fail

> Troubles and worries from the U.S. Mail
> Mailman, Mailman bring me a letter
> Something that'll tell me things are better
> Oh, U.S. Mail deliver to me
> Something that'll make me a little happ-ee.

There was some days when I'd finish three songs in one day, but those days were rare and then I'd have to sing them over and over again so I wouldn't forget them until I got back home. I always wrote them down in a special notebook and put the chords over the words. That way I'd remember 'em. I wrote a lot of songs that summer that way, just starting with something out in the fields and working with it till it got to be a full song. Sometimes Daddy would hear me singing one of my songs and ask me where I found it. One day I was singing this song:

> Well, don't tell me your troubles
> Cause I've got troubles too
> I got a broken heart, wounded pride
> And a love that won't be true
> Don't think I want to listen
> I'm not so sure I do
> Don't tell me your troubles
> Cause I've got troubles too.

I remember that look in his eyes when I told him that I'd written that song myself. It was a total surprise and he just kinda stared and then he said, "You can't write no song" and I said "I wrote that one." He just turned and walked off. Later on I'd be playing something I was writing and he'd say "You still think you're a songwriter?" or sometimes he'd just say "Cut out the racket" or "I hope you don't think you can write songs." I mostly didn't pay him no mind but sometimes I had to quit playing the guitar at home cause he would get touchy, especially when he got a few drinks in him. One time when he was drinking he even asked me "Is that a real song or did you make that up?" Lucky for me it was a real song, but it was brand new on the radio so he hadn't heard it before.

I like writing songs with a guitar the best. I'll find me a chord and start strumming on it and then move to another chord and then another one till I have a pattern. I'll try to change the chords to make it a little bit different so people won't expect what's coming and I'll keep that up until a line pops into my head and I'll sing it and see if it works and if it does then I'll try another one. Or I'll have me a line on the chorus, most likely the hook line, which will be the title, and I'll sing that until I can find something to lead up to it. Mostly I want something that will sing good. I'm always searching for words that'll fall together and fit the chords I'm strumming.

One time I was just strumming an E chord when this song came:

If you feel so all alone
That you think you can't go on
And you wonder if love can ever be real
Don't think you're by yourself
With the heartache that you felt
Cause you know the way that I feel
Feelin' that your heart
Just can't make another start
And the feelin's deep inside
Are so deep you can't describe
Well you're not the only one
Who feels troubled and alone
Cause you know the way that I feel

It isn't every day that I come up with a song. Many's the night I'll go to bed without finishing a song cause it just won't all come together but sometimes it will and I'll go to bed feeling so complete and like I'm fulfilling my purpose on earth. I feel like any day I've given the world a song is a good day for me. Sometimes I'll go back to a song I haven't finished and it will come together but sometimes I just can't get it going again. I've had to throw away a lot of songs that were almost done but something was missing and I could never find it, but when it all comes together, Lord, there ain't no better feeling on this earth. On those days I know why I've been born.

Sixteen

I come along at a good time—the 50s and early 60s—when things was getting better. Those times were certainly a lot better for me than they were for my folks in the 1920s and 30s. We got electricity when I was about four and we didn't have to burn those coal oil lamps except during storms. When I was in the fourth grade we got an indoor bathroom and that same year, 1957, we also got a TV set. It was a good year and the crops came in for good prices. Being a tobacco farmer means you only get paid once a year—in the Spring when the tobacco is sold. The rest of the time you just spend money so that one check has to last all year. It's a powerful big check—a couple thousand dollars—but it has to stretch the whole year. Course we also grew some soy beans and corn and wheat and we sold those too. We kept some pigs and cows and every now and then we'd ship some off. Ate good, though, all year round. Got milk from the cows and killed a steer every year. Killed about six hogs on a cold day in December and sold some of that meat.

Hog killing lasted all day long but other farmers helped and it was a big deal. We'd take turns going to their farms or them coming to ours. Last winter our turn came the day after Christmas.

When it was our turn, I'd get up real early in the morning, before sun-up when it was freezing cold, and start a fire under the scalding tub. That was a long iron tub about six feet long and four feet wide. We'd dig a long, shallow hole and then put that tub over it. I'd fill that tub up with water then build a fire under it so's it would get real hot. Then you go to the hog pen where the hogs'd bunch up in a corner. Actually, you wanted the hog's rear end to be in a corner and his head facing you. Then you put a twenty-two bullet right between his eyes. Daddy always did that. After the hog fell we'd put some chains around it and pull it out to the scalding pot with a tractor. That was my job.

At the scalding pot there were two parallel chains and the hog was laid on them and then lowered into the hot water. That way you could keep control and roll the hog over while he was in the water. After the skin got good and hot a bunch of us boys would get some scraping knives and scrape the hair off a that hog, then we'd cut the tendons in the back legs and stick a thick stick through them and get the hog over to some poles and hang it up and then the hog would be gutted. It was always my job to take the hog's insides up to the woods with a tractor and cart and dump them. The stomach was always like a big balloon and you learned quick never to pop that balloon cause woo-wee that smell would knock you over.

The rest of a hog killing day was spent cutting up the meat and making sausage and cutting up the fat to make lard. The fat was cut in little squares and put into an iron pot of boiling water and some rhine would float to the top and gather. You could gather that rhine up and put it in a waffle iron and oh boy that was good stuff. Called it "cracklin's" cause that's what you did after you ate it, but it sure was good. It was the ultimate gourmet treat of hog killing.

Last year it was about dark when we finished with the tractor and I was supposed to put it away in the barn where we kept it. I decided to be a hot shot and show off. I have this trick I can do where I crank up the tractor in high gear, head down to the barn and when I get to the door I push in the clutch, then hit the right wheel brake and that front end of the tractor bounces right into the barn, then I goose the throttle and gun it in. Pretty neat. But I don't ever let Daddy see me do this cause he raises holy hell whenever I do something that swell.

There were a lot of folks at our farm that day and I just had to let them see me do this so I took off down the little road to the barn. There weren't no lights on in the barn so I didn't notice one door was about half closed until I got there. It was a close call and I probably could've stopped but I thought I might make it anyway, but then right in the middle of this showing off I realized I couldn't make it and uh-oh took that door right off the hinges. All those other boys and farmers just stood around with a smirk or stupid grin on their faces while I got down off the tractor. Daddy come out of the other barn where he was making sausage and said "What's going on, here?"

Well, the first thing I said was, "If you've got a knife, I'd appreciate it if you'd put it down right now." And everybody started laughing hard as they could. He just looked madder.

"What happened?" he said again.

"Hit the barn door," I said. Everybody laughed again.

"Couldn't you see it?" he said.

"It's pretty dark," I said.

"How fast were you going?"

"Well, I wanted to hurry up so's I could get back and help you with that sausage," I said. He didn't buy that one.

"What gear did you have that tractor in?" he asked.

"Sixth," I said. That was the top speed overdrive for that old Oliver tractor. That's when he blew. Everybody stopped laughing then and turned around and walked off. I got the door back on as best I could, but it was in a lot of pieces. He was standing there screaming at me the whole time, reminding me how stupid I was to do something like that. When I finished I tried to sorta slide off into the dark.

I'm a real hot tractor driver. At least I am most of the time. I can make those tractors do all kinds of things. Like I can pop those front wheels off the ground and I can back a cart anywhere but tractors are always getting me in trouble, too. In April this year Daddy went off to the tobacco market and left me and my cousin, Thaddeus, who'd come over to visit, to take care of some chores. Well, the first thing me and Thaddeus did was each get a tractor and race from the far field to the house. We needed some water so we got off the tractors and went inside and got a jug filled up. Well you wouldn't believe it but as soon as we got back outside the house with that water then howdy doo here comes Daddy barreling down our road in his car and it's kicking up a rooster tail of dust. He slid to a stop right in front of me and Thaddeus. "What the hell are you two doing?" he said. His face was all red so I knew he needed a straight answer.

"We needed some water," I said.

"Why does it take you two tractors to get a jug of water?" he asked with both his hands on his hips.

On the back of a tractor is what you call a draw bar and that's what you hook stuff like plows, wagons, disks and carts to. Usually, when somebody is driving the tractor somebody else will stand on the draw bar, but there are these stickers with warnings about not riding on it.

"It's not really safe to stand on the draw bar," I said.

That did it. He really blew this time. Threw his hands up in the air and then flung them down and then did it again and stomped off with a red face and his mouth sputtering. Couldn't even say nothin'. Me and Thaddeus was stumped. How did he know we was racing? Come to find out he'd just gone to the next farm to pick up our neighbor, Jake Pursell. They was both going to go to the tobacco market together and that's how come he saw the whole race clear and clean across the field.

A little over a week ago, after I got out of school for the summer, Daddy had to go somewheres one morning and I was supposed to cultivate the corn. Cultivators are these things you put on a tractor that dig up the ground between the rows of a crop so the soil is worked up and loosened. Well, I didn't want to get up early so I laid in bed as long as I could while Mama kept fussing at me. I fiddle faddled around and finally got out in the field cultivating corn, but it was late in the morning so I didn't check the tractor for gas or oil or anything like you're always supposed to do so here it was just before noon dinner time and I knew Daddy'd be coming home any minute when lo and behold the fool tractor run out of gas. Run out in the field furthest from the house.

Well, I didn't want Daddy to come home and catch me not cultivating so I ran to the barn and got another tractor. That one had cultivators on it too so I hurried out to another field. This field was pretty close to the house, but it was at the opposite end of the farm from the tractor that had just run out of gas.

Sometimes when you're in a hurry you overlook things like checking the gas and I had hardly started with that other tractor—maybe done about two rows—when that fool tractor run out of gas too. As soon as it sputtered to a stop I looked up and there Daddy come driving down the road to the house. Wasn't nothing for me to do but get off that tractor and walk to the house. It was dinner time.

It was hard to tell him that I had run out of gas with both tractors the same morning and one was parked on one side of the farm and the other on the other side. He got real quiet and didn't say much, but I knew it was coming. He didn't start yelling till dinner was over and we was headed to the barn. He insulted me right regular all the way over. At the barn I went to the gas tank and got the five gallon can filled up with gas. You can bet I had to tote that heavy can every step of the way to that first tractor, even though he was walking along holding nothing. I even had to carry the funnel, too.

When that tractor was filled up I had to walk all the way back to the barn. He drove the tractor back by himself, said he'd heard it wasn't safe for somebody to ride on the draw bar. Then I had to fill up that five gallon can all over again and take it to the other tractor. Toted that can and funnel all the way by myself again. He come along and watched me put the gas in and then he went to cultivating himself after he'd said a few more choice things that nobody could've taken for compliments no matter how good their imagination was. I learned to be real careful after that and didn't run out of gas again in either one of those tractors for almost three weeks.

Seventeen

We was planning on July the Fourth being a real shindig. It fell on a Sunday that year so Mama said we had the whole day off to whoop and hollar. Daddy he didn't argue none about that so we set about making plans.

We planned on having our usual family picnic up at Grandma Gregory's house and then we'd all go down to the Fairgrounds for a fireworks show. There was also a 4-H Talent Show and I was going to be in it, playing guitar for my sister Charlene and two of her girlfriends, the Pinworth sisters, Louise and Eileen, who were going to sing. I decided that this would mark the official beginning of my show business career.

The weekend started off kinda strange when me and Daddy had to go to town first thing Saturday morning and found Peter Menningham, one of our neighbors, in his car upside down. It had run off the road and turned over. Mr. Menningham lived about two miles from us and him and his wife, Margaret, didn't have any children. They kept their place as spotless and shining as you can get a farm. That place looked like a picture on a postcard but they were kinda funny people, kept to themselves and, except at church on Sunday mornings, you'd never see 'em or hear about 'em at all. They only left St. John's County one time, back in 1946 with another couple to see Niagara Falls. Soon as they got back home they both swore they'd never leave the county again. And they didn't.

Even though it was about 8 o'clock on Saturday morning I could tell Mr. Menningham was drunk. He was laying in that car just crying like a baby. He wasn't hurt though and we got him out and some other people stopped by and soon there was a tow truck on the way. Mr. Menningham kept saying "I don't want the boy to see me like this" over and over and he was talking about me. Finally, we left and went on about our business.

We got back home just before noon dinner time and that's when we found out that Frankie Thompson and Nadine Brookline had just gotten married that very morning down at the church. Frankie was in the same grade as me and Nadine was in the grade behind me. They seemed awfully young to be getting married but I knew Frankie had been going down to see Nadine regularly and I also knew Nadine wasn't what you'd call pure as the driven snow.

A lot of boys claimed they had enjoyed her favors and also claimed that all you had to do was buy her a little present, like some candy or such, and take it to her house and then she'd take a walk with you out in the woods in back of her house. When you got back you could brag about being one of the boys and lay claim to membership in the club that had tasted the fruit of abdominal bliss, as Willie Glaser always put it. I'd never gotten around to doing it myself and then this spring it became out of the question because it would have meant being unfaithful to Kathleen Holt.

I really wanted Kathleen to see me play my guitar on July Fourth at the 4-H Talent Show because I knew she'd be impressed. Nothing impressed me more than somebody who could play the guitar real good. I figured she'd seen me play at the school Talent Show but I wasn't too good there so I decided to call her again to see if she could come down to the Fairgrounds. I didn't want to make the phone call at home cause everybody could hear me and it was still a secret romance so that meant I couldn't get to a telephone until Saturday morning, the day before the Fourth, when we got to the feed store in town after leaving Mr. Menningham.

I dialed Kathleen's number and I could tell it was her brother who answered. "Can I speak to Kathleen?" I asked. He didn't say nothing, just screamed at the top of his lungs "KATHLEEN!" Then I could hear her coming and she picked up the phone. "Hello?" she said.

"Hi, this is Compton Gregory," I said and I was getting more and more nervous every single second. I hadn't really had time to get too nervous up until then because I wasn't sure I'd even be making the call so I hadn't rehearsed what I was going to say. I made the call when I did because there happened to be a phone booth outside the feed store. When Daddy went in the store to buy some stuff I just grabbed the opportunity, jumped in and dialed her number. When she answered was when I got nervous.

She said, "Hi Compton" and her voice was kinda flat.

I swallowed real hard and then said "I was wondering if you could go out tomorrow night." Oh God, then it hit me. I didn't know how in the world I could pick her up cause I hadn't made any plans about a car or nothing.

"I'm sorry but I've got plans for tomorrow," she said. "O.K." I said. "Good-bye" and then I hung up. My palms were sweaty and I was starting to shake a little, but then I took a deep breath and walked out of that phone booth. In a few minutes I was back to normal and feeling all right again.

Saturday afternoon me and Daddy took care of some odds and ends on the farm after we got back from town, fed the animals early and went to supper. After supper, my sister Charlene and I drove down to the Pinworth girls house to rehearse. We was going to do two songs, "Cherry Pink and Apple Blossom White" and "Wolverton Mountain." I wanted to do a song of my own but nobody would let me, said I should be happy to be allowed to play behind the girls, so I worked on being thankful and practiced sneaking in a little bass run or two behind their dreadful singing.

I wanted to learn another song or two in case we got an encore but Daddy said that doing that would be thinking you was better than you are and people who got thinking they was too high and mighty were bound to fall. That's exactly what he said, "You get to thinking you're too high and mighty and you're bound to fall." Mama said we should just be thankful if nobody threw rotten tomatoes or run us off while we were doing the songs we'd planned and we shouldn't push our luck. She said it exactly like that, "Be thankful if nobody throws rotten tomatoes or runs you off. Just stick to the songs you got planned and don't push your luck."

Mama always said the Pinworth girls liked to put on hairs and that's what they did that whole practice, messing with their hair, twirling it in their fingers, acting like stars and all. We'd finish "Cherry Pink and Apple Blossom White" and they'd just primp and preen and giggle at themselves and then want to do it again, like we coulda done it any better another time. There was a mirror hanging on the side wall of what they called their parlor, which is where we practiced, and they was always glancing at themselves in that mirror. It was like they was their own audience and they loved themselves as their own biggest fans.

    We did "Cherry Pink and Apple Blossom White" in the key of A and "Wolverton Mountain" in the key of D. Mrs. Pinworth, their mama, kept complaining that I played "Cherry Pink" like it was a country song. I didn't see nothing wrong with that, plus I couldn't play it any other way. By nine that night I'd had enough of practicing and we all agreed to meet at five thirty the next night before the Talent Show started.

Eighteen

Sunday morning we got up and went to the eight o'clock service at church, which was the usual time we went to church, then on the way back home we stopped by Aunt Tootie's. Aunt Noodles was there too and all they could talk about was Frankie and Nadine. Aunt Noodles said the baby was due before Christmas and there'd been some cold days in March so Nadine probably had frost bite on her backside but Aunt Tootie said she'd heard Nadine carried a heater in her pants turned up full blast all the time and that there were scorch marks all over the ground in the woods back of her house. Said everybody was worried when Nadine walked in the woods during a dry spell cause they was afraid the woods would catch on fire and burn down. I wondered if Willie Glaser had talked to them about Nadine.

The engagement had apparently come on Thursday night when Nadine's father got the news he would be a grandfather by the end of the year. He got out his shotgun and threatened to kill 'em both unless they got married right away so the next morning they got a marriage license and blood test and then got married Saturday. Aunt Tootie said they saved a lot of money on invitations that way. Apparently only 15 people showed up for the wedding and Nadine's Daddy wasn't one of them, but when they got out of the church he was waiting there in his car and drove them to his house, which is where they're going to live until Frankie finds a job.

Willie Glaser was best man and apparently he and Nadine was cuttin' eyes at each other during the whole sacred ceremony. Aunt Tootie said that when they got outside the church Nadine walked right over to Willie and hauled off and put her fist right in his face while he was laughing. Blood started flying and Willie started cussing in front of the preacher and then Nadine kicked him in the you know what and where and he doubled over and cussed some more. Frankie just stood there until Nadine was finished and then they got into the car. Aunt Tootie said Mrs. Brookline fixed hot dogs and potato chips, which is Frankie's favorite meal, for their wedding dinner.

Aunt Noodles had gone to the wedding and said Barbara, Nadine's sister, was maid of honor and that it was the first time she'd ever seen Barbara without hair curlers. Barbara Brookline wore hair curlers everywhere, even in church on Sunday and on the bus riding to school and everybody always wondered what it was she was getting ready for, but I knew she was getting ready for her boyfriend, Tanker McGill, cause as soon as they got together she took the curlers out. The only times I'd seen Barbara without those hair curlers was when she and Tanker were together.

Aunt Tootie said that Frankie and Nadine must've had their first marital fight on Saturday afternoon cause she saw Frankie walking down the road to Wendell's store twice. They didn't have a car and Nadine's Daddy wouldn't lend them his. Said loud enough to wake the dead that the only way he'd let Frankie drive his Chevrolet was if he decided he needed some baby Chevies in the driveway. Aunt Tootie also said it was a dangerous thing for Frankie to walk that far away from Nadine with all those other boys in the neighborhood at home on a Saturday. Said it was like leaving a big pot of honey outside during a fly convention.

Mama changed the mood real quick when she asked Aunt Tootie about Uncle Elton. Aunt Tootie said the doctor told Elton he had ferocious of the liver and that if he so much as touched another single drop of alkee-hall he would die. The only way he was going to live was to stay sober so Elton was going to come over to Noodle's house for the Fourth. Since we was going over to the other side of the family's get together we didn't think we'd see Elton but just then he walked in the door.

Uncle Elton wasn't as funny as usual. He had a smile on his face but it wasn't a natural one. It was like he put a clothes hanger in his mouth to keep smiling but his heart just wasn't in it. He was sober and said yeah, the doctor said to quit drinking or else and he didn't like the or else so there he was stone cold sober and it was such a new experience that he'd stumbled and fell down twice this morning just out of habit.

Aunt Tootie offered him an iced tea and he said thank you he'd take it and would she mind if he passed out on the floor soon as he finished it and then Aunt Noodles told him he was looking good. Uncle Elton looked at her and said it wasn't nice to mislead somebody by looking at them and then talk about somebody else and then he said he couldn't see too good cause his eyes were still bloodshot and that if he cut slits under each of his eyes he'd probably bleed to death but at least he'd get a clear view before he passed on. Said he'd been looking at the world through rose colored eyeballs so long that he wasn't sure he'd recognize anybody now and he hoped he could recognize voices. Aunt Noodles said he could crack all the jokes he wanted but just don't get near any liquor. Uncle Elton said he wouldn't even drive down a road anymore if he had to go past a sign for beer, which left me wondering exactly what roads he was going to travel.

We left soon after that cause Mama had to fix some covered dishes for the Fourth of July get-together up Granny Gregory's so we went on home where Daddy read the newspaper funnies while Mama and Charlene gathered up food and stuff. The men folks all wanted the feed to start at 12 noon cause that was dinner time.

Them Gregorys are funny that way. They can eat a full meal at 11 o'clock on the morning but when noon comes around they want to eat a full meal again. They say if it's 12 o'clock noon then it's dinner time and that means food. At 12 o'clock noon all them Gregorys automatically got hungry, whether they'd eaten just before or not.

Nineteen

When we got to Granny Gregory's the place was hopping. Uncle Roadkill, who lived with Granny, had gotten drunk the night before, then got up Sunday morning and started drinking again to curb his hangover, or so he said, and that meant he'd missed church and Granny Gregory didn't want nobody to miss church. It was like a spiritual crisis when Granny had to be in the same house on a Sunday with somebody who hadn't gone to church, like lightning was going to strike or something. She just felt real uneasy about missing church if'n she wasn't deathly ill.

Church wasn't exactly on Uncle Roadkill's mind that morning. He said he'd repent later but that now was the time for glorious sin and he wanted sin enough to make repentance worthwhile. Uncle Roadkill always said don't do nothing half way. If you're going to get drunk, get roaring drunk. Uncle Roadkill wasn't no hypocrite; he practiced what he preached.

When we arrived at Grandma's, Uncle Roadkill was in right rare form, yelling about this and that. Mostly politics about Lyndon Johnson coddling the coloreds and Martin Luther King ruining the country and everybody was looking out for the niggers but wasn't nobody looking out for people like him. Said being free, white and twenty-one should have some meaning and be like it used to be. To hear Uncle Roadkill tell it, being free, white and twenty-one should be all a man needed and now it didn't mean a thing. In fact, it was held against you and that was reason enough to get snot flying drunk on the Fourth of July.

Uncle Soup and Aunt Fussie—if ever there was a name that fit a woman perfect it was her's—got there with their twin boys, J. T. and Randy and daughter Shirley first and Uncle Soup and Uncle Roadkill got into a big argument pretty quick. Not about politics, though. They kept agreeing about that and adding on to what the other said, which kept it from being a full blown fist fight, but Uncle Soup wanted a snort and Aunt Fussie didn't want him to have one. Uncle Roadkill said he didn't have any more booze and Uncle Soup said he was lying and hiding it somewhere. At first Granny just said "Why don't you two just drink some gasoline and then smoke a cigarette" but then she started saying "Now you two quit" while she put the table cloths and plastic forks on the picnic table.

This argument was going on real good when we got there. First thing Mama said when we drove up was "Looks like Roadkill got a head start on everybody else" and the next thing she said was "Catnip, you steer clear of Roadkill. You know he's gonna want to pick a fight or get you riled up. Don't let him get your goat." Daddy he just nodded and said "Looks like somebody cut the grass here yesterday."

Soon as we drove up Uncle T-Bone and Aunt Tootie pulled up with their kids and Thaddeus, their oldest, jumped out and said, "I've got some firecrackers." Aunt Tootie said, "Thaddeus, you better not shoot them off around the little kids. Somebody could get hurt."

We was all piling out of the two cars and soon as Daddy got out and straightened up he said, "Now you kids run on and play" but Mama said, "Dinner will be ready soon so stay close" cause she was carrying the covered dishes inside and then Uncle Bubba and Aunt Irene came with their kids. That meant there was ten cousins and one sister for me to occupy my time with, but they was all younger than me. Used to be I didn't mind it so much, them being younger and all. In fact we played together real good, but I was 16 years old now and I just didn't want to play games with a bunch of kids anymore so I just sorta wandered over by the garden fence while the cousins all headed out to the field in front of the house and started playing tag. The grown-ups was gathered under the two big oak trees in the front yard.

Uncle Roadkill had a good head of steam on him and he was turning mean. He was walking around the yard and Uncle Soup was walking around behind him saying "Where's the damn bottle, Roadkill? I know you're hiding it from me" and Uncle Roadkill kept saying "I ain't got no damn bottle. It's all gone." The women folk was putting out the spread and finally Granny said, "Time to eat!" Well, you'd a thought a herd of buffalo had answered the call with everybody rushing in but first we had to say grace and Granny asked Bubba to say it. That insulted Roadkill who said "I live here so I'll say the grace." Granny was uneasy with that cause she felt it was not good policy to ask someone on the outs with God to ask His blessing. She wasn't exactly sure how He'd respond and Granny always said that if you didn't say a sincere grace before a meal then you'd choke on your food.

There wasn't no arguing with Roadkill at a time like that but Uncle Soup tried. "You're too damn drunk," he said. "Who's drunk?" said Roadkill. "I've drank more than this and gone to work." Then Soup said again, "You can't ask the Lord's blessing when you're drunk" and Roadkill shot right back "I ain't that drunk" then T-Bone up and says, "Let Roadkill say the blessing and then Bubba will add on anything he might've forgot." Roadkill didn't like that idea much but his brain was too cloudy to come up with an answer. It was a complex problem for a man in Roadkill's condition to puzzle out.

Roadkill was actually in a terrible dilemma. On one hand he was joyfully drunk and happy to brag about it but, on the other hand, if someone accused him of being drunk he would deny it and was ready to get in a fist fight to prove the other person wrong. On the spiritual side, Roadkill was defiantly out of sorts with the Lord and wallowing gloriously in the sin of drunkeness. On the other side of that same coin, he knew he couldn't say grace without repenting first and he was just not ready for repentance.

There was deathly silence for a little while and then Roadkill said, "Lord, I thank you I'm free, white and twenty-one" and then he fell face forward right on the ground. Stone cold passed out. It was a miracle he missed the table. Later, after everybody had commented about it being a miracle Roadkill missed the table Mama said it was miracle the Lord put the ground where it was otherwise Roadkill would've fallen all the way to China.

When Roadkill fell out, Granny never missed a beat. She just said, "Bubba, you finish the grace" and Bubba said "Lord, I'm also thankful I'm free, white and twenty-one and we thank you for this food and pray it's fittin' to eat. Amen."

Well, that prayer didn't set too well with the women folk. They didn't feel a prayer was needed to make their food fittin' to eat. They'd worked long and hard on that food and they knew it was good so Bubba was on the outs by the time the meal started.

The whole family dug in and filled up their plates. Them paper plates get squishy and bend with hot food on them so everybody was trying to balance what they had and find a place to eat what they got. It's a big family so there was people all over the yard and inside Granny's house eating. Daddy and Mama ate in the house cause it was easier to keep the flies away inside and, like Daddy says, nobody in their mind wants to be outside on a hot day anyway. Even in the shade. Daddy always thought the dumbest thing in the world was some girls who would lay out in the sun during the day. He always said if you had to be outside on a hot day, and you could choose, then you should always sit in the shade. Those girls didn't have to even be outside in the first place and then they parked themselves right in the hot sun so that made them double dumb in Daddy's eyes. For Mama it was not coming in out of the rain that signified dumbness; for Daddy it was laying out in the sun. Between the two of them they had the criteria for dumbness established in relation to the weather. Neither one of them ever talked about dumbness and snow as far as I remember.

Actually, I had to agree with Daddy on his views in one way cause I spent a lot of time out in the fields on a tractor with that hot sun beating down on me and it sure was a relief to get to the shade, but I also knew at school that the girls worked hard on their tans and girls like Patty Sherman always struck a fetching figure when they was tanned. It was a big deal with them so I figured what's the harm, let 'em lay out in the sun. I didn't think the Norwood family was too smart though. There were three Norwood girls, Talulah, Annette and Natalie, and they were all real fair skinned which meant they didn't tan, they burnt. Their Mama always made 'em sit out in the sun though and bleached their hair, which was real blonde anyway, and put lemon juice on it cause she thought they would all be movie stars someday. She knew all about every movie star in the world cause she always bought all those magazines that told about what movie stars did, but I always thought her girls were all too ugly to be movie stars and walking around beet red all summer didn't add any to their looks in a movie star kind of way.

Twenty

Nobody talked much while they was eatin' except Aunt Tootie. Somehow Aunt Tootie could talk a mile a minute even while she was eating and never talk with her mouth full. I still don't know how she done it. Nobody bothered Uncle Roadkill, who stayed in the same place he fell for the rest of the afternoon, except every now and then he'd groan or fart and roll around a bit. We all just stepped over him when we wanted more food.

By the time everybody was finished eating, all the grown-ups had gathered in the kitchen, which was the biggest room in Granny's house. They all sat around the table, which was actually two tables put together. That made nine adults in that room. The next room, which was just off the kitchen where Granny kept her freezer, was a table where six kids sat and the rest were scattered in the living room or outdoors.

We all ate until we couldn't eat no more. When Granny puts on a feed it's always something else. That's what Mama always said. She said, "When Granny puts on a feed it's always something else." Granny makes the best potato salad in the entire universe and her biscuits taste like the Heavenly Feast. Aunt Tootie always said that at the Lord's final banquet He's gonna ask Granny to do the cookin' and when this world breaks bread the final time it'll be Granny's biscuits they're breaking cause nobody makes 'em any better. When Tootie said that Granny just said "Oh you shush" and "I hope those biscuits are fittin' to eat this time" all the while knowin' she'd topped herself again.

Actually, Granny's biscuits have gotten her in trouble in the past cause Granny has the sugar diabetes inside her and she's also way overweight. Granny is four feet eleven inches tall and almost as big around as she is tall so the doctor made her cut down on her biscuits. Granny used to eat 12 biscuits at every meal but the doctor told her she could only have one. Well, Granny only made that one biscuit for herself to eat but she made it as big as the pan.

Right after dinner Uncle T-Bone went out to the trunk of his car and got out a big wash tub filled with beer and ice and put it under the tree, then the men folk would send one of their kids out to get 'em a beer and they sat around a table talking until they got to the point where they just sat there and drank and nobody said anything unless they needed a beer.

After the men folk parked themselves around the table and started drinking, then the women folk drifted out to the front yard. They couldn't sit at the picnic table cause Uncle Roadkill was still laying there, although he didn't cause much trouble passed out and all, except he snored and farted quite a bit, but the women all took their lawn chairs and moved away from him a little and commenced to gabbin'.

Us kids didn't want to be step'n'fetchit's all afternoon, which is what we'd a been if we'd hung around the house. Everytime one of the men wanted a beer he'd start callin' out kids names until he found one that would come, then he'd send 'em out to the tub for a can of beer. That got old in a hurry.

Me and the cousins went out back of Granny's house to the barns and started playing hide'n'seek and then somebody—I'm pretty sure it was Thaddeus—decided we should ride Old Mister. Mister is the meanest horse you can imagine, real high spirited, and he likes to bite. He was in the small pen but we got him into his stall by putting some grain there. Thaddeus managed to get the bridle on, then he held the bridle while I got the saddle on. Charlene crawled along the top of the fence and plopped herself in the saddle before I'd actually finished tightening the cinch.

By that time Mister had figured out what was going on and decided to take action. Thaddeus had just opened the gate to Mister's stall and the horse spun around and kicked me with both its' hooves. I managed to turn to the side but he put two big bruises on the side of my hip and leg. Then Mister bolted out a that stall and took off out the barnyard. We'd left every gate open so he run right down the road towards the woods. Charlene was on his back hanging on for dear life with her arms wrapped around his neck. Nine cousins took off after Mister with me coming along limping. It hurt so bad I wanted to cry, but I'd grown too big and was too old for it so I had to hold it all in and run after Charlene and Mister.

Mister run over a mile before he finally stopped in the middle of the woods. When we finally caught up with him he was standing there in the woods and Charlene had slid off and was sitting on a log crying. We all got there and made sure Charlene was all right and then I asked her, "Why didn't you pull one rein?" cause everybody knows if you pull on a single rein the horse will just go in circles until he stops. "I didn't want to hurt his mouth," Charlene said. Well, that was about the most fool thing I'd ever heard. Here this horse had almost kilt her running away and she was worried about hurting his mouth. But that was Charlene.

Thaddeus got on Mister to ride him back to the barn and the rest of us started walking back. We hadn't taken twelve steps when we run into the women folk all running toward us saying "What happened? What happened? Is everybody all right?" Well, of course we were and we told them that. Then we told them about Charlene and Mister and they all said we didn't have no business fooling with that horse anyway and we should put it up before somebody or other got hurt. Well, it was too late for that and Thaddeus told them about me getting kicked so they wanted me to drop my pants and show 'em where I'd been kicked. Fat chance of that. I just told 'em I was fine but Mama kept saying "If you're fine, why are them horse prints on your pants?" I said I wanted to wear a horseshoe for good luck.

We walked back towards the barns and pretty soon we run into the men folk a-walking down the road kinda slow and woozy and they all asked the same questions the women folk asked, so we had to give 'em the same answers all over again and then they told us we didn't have no business fooling with that horse anyway and we should put it away before somebody or other got hurt. We reckon'd we'd gotten that message pretty good.

Back at the house the men folk went back into the kitchen after each pulled out a cold beer from the tub. The women folk sat back down in their lawn chairs under the tree. Us kids went back to the barns and I'm pretty sure it was Thaddeus again who came up with the idea of having a dog show.

Granny didn't like any dogs out running loose cause they always killed her turkeys and chickens. Not that her turkeys and chickens were any great prizes. Granny's turkeys and chickens weren't covered with feathers like normal turkeys and chickens; instead, they had patches of feathers all over them and then there were bare spots. County agents from five different counties had come up to Granny's looking at those birds but nobody could figure out why they were the way they were.

We used to have chickens ourselves until we started raising bird dogs. Them bird dogs would stand those chickens—they was pointers so they'd just point—but the chickens kept moving around and pretty soon the bird dogs got tired of pointing and ate the chickens. We lost every single chicken that way. Granny didn't want that to happen to her's.

Uncle Roadkill had two bird dogs and two rabbit dogs in four pens in the back of the corn house, plus there was an old mongrel dog that was part collie and part everything else chained on the side of the house. Aunt Ilene had a little Chihuahua that she always carried in her lap and Earlene, Ilene's daughter, went and got that dog, which was named "Cha-Cha-Cha."

All the dogs had collars so we got some twine out of the tractor shed to use as leashes and we took those six dogs out into the field beside the barn for the contest. Thaddeus was going to be the judge and I was the announcer. Everybody else had a dog, except the twins, J. T. and Randy, who acted like they was one person anyway, and the first thing everybody was supposed to do was make all them dogs sit. Well, you might as well been trying to teach a pig to sing, as Mama said later, as try to get any of those dogs to sit down, much less them do it all together at the same time.

Since they wouldn't sit Thaddeus decided we'd have a race and got them all lined up in a row and lit one of his firecrackers that he'd brought along. Instead of running in a straight line down to where I was standing to decide the winner, the dogs all took off after each other. The twine got wrapped around everybody's legs and burned, so everybody let the twine go and then the dogs got in a massive fight that would've made the Middle East look peaceful, as Mama observed later. It was the most God awful mess you could ever imagine and us cousins were right in the middle of it trying to sort it all out.

Actually, the girl cousins were mostly screaming with Earlene yelling "Cha-Cha-Cha! Cha-Cha-Cha!" while the little Chihuahua ran underneath all the other dogs yipping and biting their legs and tails. The big dogs never could find the little rat, as Daddy called him, so they'd get bit by the Chihuahua and then start a fight with another big dog. About that time the women folk came running again with Ilene crying "Cha-Cha-Cha, Cha-Cha-Cha!" She finally dived into that pile of dogs and picked up the little rat. Ilene had tears coming down her face while she hugged that poor excuse for a dog, all the while saying "My poor little Cha-Cha-Cha, my poor little Cha-Cha-Cha" and then she started talking baby talk to the dog, "Is'm oo all wights wittle Cha-Cha-Cha? Are you's okey dokey my wittle presh-us." It was enough to make you want to fwow up.

Meanwhile, her own kids were spinning around from the twine wrapped around their legs and the women folk were all fussing. That's when we saw the men come walking out the house. They was a little wobbly but they came along fairly steady, wiping their mouths with their arms and spittin' every now and then. Uncle Bubba was cleaning his ears with his car keys. It was the usual questions, "What's going on here?" "What happened?" and the usual answers, "I don't know" and "We was having a Dog Show." Then Uncle T-Bone asked "Whose stupid idea was this anyway?" and Thaddeus said, real quick, "Compton's."

Actually, what I had said earlier was that we should do something other than sit around or play hide'n'seek but it was Thaddeus who come up with the specific idea of a Dog Show. All the men turned on me and Daddy looked straight hard at me and said, "I knew if it was a stupid idea it must've been yours!" Then Uncle Bubba said, "Compton, you ain't got the sense God gave a goose" and then Uncle Soup said, "Catnap, I wouldn't lay claim on him for mine" and then Uncle T-Bone said "You shouldn't have put all these little kids in danger like this. Somebody could'a got hurt" and then Daddy said, "If somebody had'a got hurt, then what would you do?"

I just stood there trying to figure out how to tell the truth but I knew it wasn't no use. Their minds had already been made up about the truth and facts would only make 'em mad so I just kept quiet. I did give Thaddeus a hard look but he turned quick and headed back to the house.

I think he wanted to get me back for teaching him the grown up word "shit," which is what we kids were taught to call "poo poo." A few years back I'd showed him some cow poop and told him that grown-ups called it "shit." I knew that cause I'd heard 'em say it out loud myself. So he's with Daddy and the uncles and they're walking across the cow pasture and he said "Don't step in that shit" and they asked him who told him that word and he said I did. The men folk laughed about it, but when they told Mama and the aunts they all whupped Thaddeus and washed his mouth out with soap and told him never to learn anything I taught him again.

All us kids headed back to the house while the men folk set about sorting out the dogs and getting them back to the house, which is not easy to do with that much beer in you. I know Daddy wanted to whup me but he had to get the dogs straightened out so I took the opportunity to be somewhere else. I went back to the car and got out my guitar and went off to myself and started strumming. That's what I was doing when five o'clock rolled around and Charlene said it was time to go to the Talent Show.

Twenty-One

The 4-H Talent Show started at 6 p.m. and it was advertised as a big deal because they was bringing in a big star, Gary Garrison, who was a disc jockey on the radio station, to be the master of ceremonies. I heard he was getting $50 to do this, which was big money just to say howdy to a crowd and inform an audience of parents that it was their own child they was watching on stage.

We got to the Fairgrounds about quarter after five and I tuned up my guitar and that's when I heard about Fudge-Dip getting killed. First, let me explain about Fudge-Dip's name. See, there wasn't nothing worse than being called a nigger lover. That would get you in a fight quicker than anything but Fudge-Dip and his brother, Chocko, which was short for Chocolate, called each other nigger lovers all the time and then they changed it to Fudge-dip and Chocko. They used to fight about it but gradually just settled into the names and used them all the time and saved "nigger lover" for special occasions when they was real mad at each other.

Fudge-Dip and Chocko had both been born the same year, Fudge-Dip in January and Chocko in November, one year before I was born. They came from a family with twenty-three kids, of which twenty survived. The other three died as infants. Fudge-Dip and Chocko's Daddy was a local handy man who would come around and fix most anything, although Uncle T-Bone used to say the only tools he owned was a hammer and crow bar and that was how he fixed everything.

Fudge-Dip and Chocko had been out drinking on the Fourth with Tub Dillingham, who was kinda fat and that's how he got his name. Tub was driving and they was trying to see how fast they could go around Dead Man's Curve, which was at the bottom of Rip Gut Hill. Uncle T-Bone said he heard they was doing 100 miles an hour when the car flipped over and Fudge-Dip, who was in the middle of the front seat, flew out the window. Said you couldn't even recognize him when it was over and he'd finished sliding down that highway.

Well, that just about turned my stomach cause I knew Fudge-Dip, although we weren't good friends. Matter of fact, I hated him, but it was a shock to know he was dead. He was mean and I would've felt better if he'd only been permanently injured. Anyway, it's hard to concentrate on giving a sterling performance in a Talent Show when you've just heard that somebody you know has died.

There were eleven acts on the 4-H Talent Show and we was fifth. We all played outside on the back of a flat-bed truck, which I thought was pretty neat. The Disc Jockey tried to be funny and yukked it up between acts. Frankly, somebody should've paid him $50 to shut up but thinking about that money increased my desire to enter show business, seeing how it was such easy money and there was no work involved.

I wished that me and Billy Boy Lindsley could'a entered this Talent Contest. We'd talked about it and both of us wanted to. We both thought that if we did a song that showed off our harmony singing we had a pretty good chance of winning, but Daddy and Mama didn't want me and Billy Boy to play together. Mama said that Charlene had never been in a Talent Show before and I'd been in one at school and that she should have the opportunity, too. I said that Charlene and the Pinworth girls could just sing by themselves or let Eileen Pinworth play the piano. She'd been taking lessons since Moses walked across the lake but Mama said the girls needed me to play with them and that she was sure it would sound better than anything me and Billy Boy could come up with.

Then I asked if I could be in two acts—I'd play for the girls and then me and Billy Boy would perform—but Mama said she thought that was against the rules and that I needed to stick to just one act. She also said that if I was on the stage twice people would get tired of seeing me. That's exactly what she said, "If you get up on that stage twice, people will get tired of seeing you." She also said being up there twice people would think I was trying to hog the spotlight. She said it just like that, "People will think you're trying to hog the spotlight." I asked Daddy what he thought about it and he just said, "I'll bet there's gonna be a pretty good crowd for the fireworks afterward" so that's why me and Billy Boy didn't play at the Fourth of July Talent Show.

The first act on the 4-H Talent Show was a tap dancer, the second was a four-piece band that played "Louie Louie" and made everybody mad by performing pornography at a family show. That's what a lot of people said about that song but I could never make heads or tails of the lyrics so I can't say for certain. The next act was a little kid who recited a poem, the fourth was a guy who did "Mack the Knife" by himself and forgot the words in the middle of the song. He just stood there and scratched his head and then stomped his foot and then he'd swing his right arm and snap his fingers like gosh golly and put his hand on his hip and look away with his other hand on his forehead while his foot was a'patting. Then he'd start over and forget again. I'd a pulled the curtain down on him but there wasn't no curtain to pull. The fourth time he tried he remembered the whole thing after his mother yelled the words at him in a whisper.

We was fifth and did "Cherry Pink and Apple Blossom White" and then "Wolverton Mountain" without saying a word. We was introduced as "a girl trio" called "The Cuties" like I wasn't even there. Nobody had talked to me about billing and if they had I wouldn't have gone for that idea. If they wanted a potted plant then just let 'em find one that can play the guitar.

As a matter of fact I did better than the girls did, thank you very much, cause I kept my rhythm and played the right chords and never stopped when they messed up. Two sang one set of words and the other sang something else twice. And I also played in the same key the whole time. That's more than I can say for them cause they changed keys without me from one verse to the next in "Cherry Pink" and that ain't the way we rehearsed it. I say if you're going to modulate you better let your guitar player know about it. They didn't so I stuck to my guns and finished where I started, which they also managed to do after rolling their eyes back at me a time or two.

We all finished fourth. The first prize winner was a band that played last and did "Jailhouse Rock" just like the record. Boy, they was good and that's how they got on last. Second place went to a skinny guy with a banjo who sang "Mrs. Brown You've Got a Lovely Daughter." Third was a girl who sang "Downtown" while her mother played the piano.

After the Talent Show the winning band, The Impalas, played for awhile and then we watched the fireworks go off over the Fairgrounds. Nobody laid down to watch the fireworks because it was considered more proper to stand, I guess, and because if somebody had-a laid down they wouldn't've been able to see anything with everybody else standing. It would've probably been pretty dangerous too with the crowd there and somebody would've no doubt come along and tripped over you or stumbled and fallen on you. Especially since it was dark and they'd set a record for beer sales that day.

I was watching the fireworks like everybody else, standing beside Louise Pinworth and we were chatting every now and then about the usual, you know "Oh, isn't that a pretty one" or "I like it when three go off." I had quit looking for Kathleen Holt in the crowd. I looked hard during the Talent Show, and especially during the time we played, but hadn't seen hide nor hair of her.

Well, Louise was standing close anyway and then she said she was getting a bit chilly, even though it was a July night, and so she got right up beside me to keep warm she said and then she started looking up at me and kept talking about fireworks and my guitar playing, which she said she admired and which added considerably to their performance. I had to look down to see into her face to answer back when, lo and behold, I looked down and our faces were like inches apart. When I didn't look back up quick she just sorta leaned into me and it was like metal and magnet I reckon.

Well, she kissed me right on the lips real light and I didn't move and then she came again, put her lips on mine and put her tongue inside my mouth. Lordy, Lordy, Lordy. I tingled all over and fireworks went off in my brain and the rest of my body. I never knew people kissed like that cause that sure wasn't the way Mama ever kissed me. None of the aunts neither, but I took to it right quick and enjoyed it so much I didn't want to stop. While that whole crowd was looking up at fireworks, me and Louise Pinworth had our own fireworks going off inside our own mouths. Boy could she kiss.

Well, our kissing went on until the fireworks were over and then we headed back towards the parking lot. It was a bit difficult for me to walk my usual way. We got to her car and said good-bye but didn't kiss cause there was too many other people around, although that certainly did not stop us, or even occur to us, in the midst of the fireworks display because time had stood still and rushed on past us. Then I walked over to where our car was parked.

I was feeling like I'd just learned the world's greatest secret and had special knowledge; at the same time, I felt like a dumb fool for not knowing people kissed like this before. I still wasn't sure if it was generally accepted by everybody or whether it was limited to a special group with special knowledge or whether it was alright to kiss like this out in public or not. I didn't think so because I hadn't seen anybody else do that. Then again, I missed a lot of stuff. Mama always said I lived in a world of my own and most of the time I didn't even know the rest of the world was going by, but I sure caught up on a new style of kissing that night and couldn't wait to do it again.

Then it struck me that I'd been unfaithful to Kathleen Holt and I felt terrible guilty. At the same time, I knew how to kiss her if I ever got the chance, although I wasn't sure if that was a polite kind of kissing to be tried with a high class girl like Kathleen or not. Maybe I'd hold back kissing her like that for awhile, then I'd let her know I was a man of the world at the proper time.

That night when I got in bed I thought about kissing a lot and practiced solo just moving my own tongue around in my mouth. Next time, I would be prepared. I kept feeling guilty about being unfaithful to Kathleen; at the same time, I was grateful to Louise for showing me how to kiss. I tried to imagine kissing Kathleen that way but it just didn't seem to fit. Besides, every time I thought about real kissing it was Louise's face and mouth that was there. I figured I'd better practice some more with Louise before I kissed Kathleen like that. If Kathleen asked I would tell her I wasn't being unfaithful by kissing Louise, I was just practicing so I could get it right for her.

Twenty-Two

Fudge-Dip's death wasn't all the bad news that July Fourth. Happy Harwell had gotten drunk and gone out in his boat and then fell overboard and the motor ran over him and cut him up. The doctors had to amputate his left arm. Lucky for him he was right-handed. That was a little bit better than what happened to Perry Hammerick last fall cause he had to have his right arm amputated when he got it caught in a corn picker. Perry didn't shut the machine off when it got jammed and he was pulling out corn stalks when the machine pulled him in. You could hear him hollering for miles before somebody got there and shut it off.

There were some other things too, mostly from drinking too much. Lydell Lacy was in jail cause he'd gotten drunk and put his fist through a window down at The River View Tavern and Delbert Longworth was in jail for shooting at his wife, Arlene. Big news from the high and mighty was that Laverne Prince, otherwise known as Mrs. Halton Prince, whose husband is head of the Volunteer Fire Department and a Big Wheel in town, had run off with Robert Chavrinsky, a State Trooper. I heard she got up on the Fourth before Halton did and got dressed and he thought she was going to the early church service, which was strange cause they usually went to the late service together. She left and never came back that day.

Halton got real irritated when his dinner wasn't ready at noon and had an all points bulletin put out about four that afternoon. That's when the dispatcher told him the news. Laverne Prince is one good looking woman and I don't see how Halton, as ugly as he is, will ever replace her with anything comparable.

The biggest tragedy of that day, and the one that hit me the hardest, was that Russell Davidson, who would've graduated from high school in June except he got into some trouble and the judge told him either to go in the Army or go to jail and so he went in the Army, had been killed in Viet Nam. I knew him cause he used to play on our baseball team. News arrived at his parent's house on the morning of July Fourth and I heard about it at the Fairgrounds after the Talent Show.

I'd heard about Viet Nam on the news but hadn't paid too much attention to it. I'd heard Russell had been sent there but didn't think too much about that, either. I remembered the last time I ever saw Russell Davidson was in April when he got home from the Army training and he told me then he'd got his orders for Viet Nam. I remember that he looked scared when he told me.

Russell Davidson's funeral was held on Tuesday, July 13 and I heard a lot about Viet Nam in the meantime. It sounded like a mess to me, but everybody said we had to be there so I believed 'em. Uncle Roadkill, who had been in the Army in World War II, said there was no greater honor than to die for your country. I don't believe that's the way Melvin Davidson, Russell's father looked at it. During the funeral he cried like a baby.

There was a lot of people in that church and it struck me that I was going to a funeral of somebody who could've been me. I felt a lot older that day cause Russell was about my age and I knew what it must feel like to know somebody your whole life and then they die and you have to go to their funeral. A lot of old people do that all the time but I didn't exactly relish the experience. Matter of fact, I went to Fudge-Dip's funeral too, about a week before, but that was different. First, I didn't like Fudge-Dip and second he'd brought on his own death and third, people dying in car wrecks was more normal that somebody dying over somewhere you'd never heard of before.

At the funeral the preacher talked about being thankful for the time we had spent with Russell and that we were all safe from Communists in Asia because Russell gave his life and that we can never understand God's ways but we must accept them anyway. Well, he was certainly right about not understanding God's ways, but I hadn't really felt in danger before from Communists in Asia and didn't feel any safer than I already was just because Russell was dead. That whole line of logic was dubious at best, as one of my teachers used to say. Still, I believed what I heard and what I heard was that this country was in trouble and the Communists were coming and we'd better stop 'em now or else they'd be at our back door soon and they'd be a whole lot harder to stop there. I knew the best thing for me to do was hate Communists and stand against them but my feelings about that war was mixed up right then. I didn't like the Viet Nam war a single bit, but I had been convinced that it was necessary.

There wasn't a shade tree around the spot where they buried Russell in the little cemetery just across from Mabel Carlton's house. It was the church cemetery but it was about a mile away from the church in a field that used to belong to Gorman Klein's farm. Six of Russell's uncles were the pall bearers and they brought the casket over to the grave. We stood there in the hot sun and a few words were said and then three guys dressed up in uniforms that had come down from Washington D. C. that morning raised their rifles and shot them off up into the sky. They folded up the flag on Russell's coffin into a triangle and gave it to Melvin Davidson, who had stopped crying by then, and we all walked away, back to our own lives. It felt eerie cause the sun was still shining and grass was still growing and trees were there and there was a rabbit at the edge of the woods and a turtle at the edge of the road and some birds flying around. It was like nothing was out of the ordinary. Life was still going on but it also felt like life had stopped, too. I couldn't understand how I could be so full of sadness while all of nature acted like nothing was wrong or out of the ordinary.

Russell was important to his family and friends but he wasn't important to this world. Nobody is. I don't care who you are, how big or important you are or high and mighty, when you die the world's still gonna keep on turning. Birds and rabbits and turtles ain't even gonna notice, much less pay attention or act different. It's just another day in the life of God.

Twenty-Three

I knew I was going to be a singer and songwriter in the sixth grade. I don't really know how I knew, but I just knew and it scared me cause nobody else in our family had ever been a singer and songwriter and I didn't know how singers or songwriters made money or anything, but it was just something I couldn't get rid of, though Lord knows I tried. Even joined the "Future Business Leaders" club in high school trying to shake it and be respectable but I only met with the "Future Business Leaders" club once to get our picture taken for the yearbook. The rest of the time they was holding bake sales or car washes or selling candy bars or stuff like that and none of that appealed to me. Being a business leader didn't seem like it would be all that tough but the kind of stuff they did was annoying. It just wasn't my line of work.

In the sixth grade Mrs. Fenworth announced the Daughters of the American Revolution was having a contest for the best writing so I wrote a poem. Wasn't much to it, I guess, but I seemed to have a knack for it and I liked it and it really set me apart from the other kids.

The kids in class were amazed I could write stuff like that but Mrs. Fenworth never liked me so she didn't tell me the due date for the contest, which kept me from entering the contest and, incidentally, also kept the likes of me from polluting her beloved DAR. She was a mean woman and also the one that fixed it so's I couldn't win the Mr. May Day contest.

See, what it was was a May Day celebration and there was a King and Queen from the sixth grade that walked down this long grassy slope at school and sat up on the stage while everybody else from the school did these dances and skits and other such nonsense. The class voted for five boys and five girls and I was one of the boys. So was

Leonard West, her pet and one of the five girls was Patty Sherman and every guy in the class was in love with her.

Well, ole Mrs. Fenworth just couldn't stand to see some sharecropper's kid walking beside the beautiful and popular Patty Sherman so she announces to the class that she's decided to have them vote for a couple that she's matched up by height so it would look better. She matched me with Fayrene Stoneman, whose daddy was also a sharecropper. Fayrene is a sweet, real quiet girl but she didn't have a prayer of winning, which meant I didn't either and so Patty Sherman and Leonard West marched down that grassy slope as King and Queen of May Day, even though Patty was almost a head taller than Leonard.

Nobody liked Leonard West. He was a real twerp, always pulling crap then running to the teacher and telling on somebody so they'd get into trouble and he'd be the teacher's pet. Mrs. Fenworth ate that up and loved that little prick to pieces, but no boy in that class respected him cause of the way he was. Actually, all the guys were amazed at ole Leonard for one thing, though.

Leonard West could pee further than any kid I ever knew. He'd stand way back from the urinal in the bathroom and pee this big, long arc that landed in a perfect bulls eye and then as he was peeing he'd walk forward in little steps so's he'd be standing right by the urinal when he ran out of steam and finished up. It was amazing to see and he did it every bathroom break. We got kinda tired of watching this spectacle but it was Leonard's claim to fame and the only way he could stay one of the boys so we admired his single talent all through the sixth grade.

The other thing Mrs. Fenworth did that really made me mad was in the reading contest. First, she made this contest where you'd get a star on a chart for every book you read. Man, I went to town and out-read everybody. But Mrs. Fenworth changed the rules—said I'd read too many "short" books—which were mostly the same books everybody else was reading—and that I'd read too much biography (which was my favorite) and not enough of a wide selection and then finally just took down the chart and didn't give no prizes. Then we all took one of those reading tests and I scored higher than anybody in the class. It said I was reading at a high school level in the sixth grade. There was another test that would show I could read at the level of a high school graduate and I wanted to take it but Mrs. Fenworth wouldn't let me. Said it was useless and it didn't matter cause I wasn't going to amount to nothing nohow, having my background and all. It would just be a waste of her time. She wanted for some of the other kids to take that test but when they didn't get scores better than mine she dropped the whole idea.

Boy, I'll tell you something, reading saved me. Caught onto it quick somehow, even though they put me in the slowest group of kids when I started school. The school people said they just didn't think I should be with the top group of kids in the first grade cause I probably wasn't as smart as them, but I caught on quick and they couldn't keep me out of that top group so they had to put me in there, but they wouldn't move me up until the next grade.

I got so frustrated in that slow reading group in the first grade cause I read everything I was supposed to and then read the top group's books. We had to sit in these chairs in the front of the room every day and read out of a book to the teacher. There were two rows in a semi-circle. Well, there were some scissors on a shelf right behind the desk where I sat and one day I picked up one of those scissors and cut my pants all up. It was fun to cut cloth and I kept doing it and those pants ended up in tatters. Well, it came time to read so I had to get up and I tried to find a spot on the back row but they was all taken so I had to sit on the front row. Miss Owens, the teacher, took one look at me and her mouth fell open.

I never really knew why I did that. It seemed like fun at the time and I never thought about what would happen later, like when I stood up. After that I started thinking now and then when I was doing something about how I'd explain it later. It was a good lesson. Made me think ahead and work up an explanation in the midst of some deviltry and even kept me out of deviltry clear and clean some other times.

In the sixth grade I wrote stuff for other kids, like poems to go along with their papers and stuff. Even wrote papers for other kids, especially book reports. That got tough cause a lot of guys would make up the name of a book like *Drag Racing in America* or *The Art of Wrestling* and then come to me to write up a book report on it so they could hand it in. Of course, the teacher had never heard of the books, which didn't exist anyway, and she'd certainly never read them. Didn't check either, but it was tough on me cause I had to make up a whole story line and everything. On a required book like *The Scarlet Letter* I'd write my own report and then a bunch of others, but I made sure they weren't as good as mine.

In high school I kept writing and wrote three books. Actually it was three spiral notebooks I filled up with notes and stories and jokes and ideas and just whatnot. Sent them off to a New York publisher just after school finished this year and they came back like a rubber ball. I'm amazed they even sent them back, wondered why they didn't throw them in the trash or something. I didn't tell nobody I'd sent them off. Wanted to surprise everybody, I guess. Besides, if anybody knew they'd just make fun of me trying to be something I wasn't or thinking I was better than I am or could do something that I should've known better than to even try.

Anyway, those New York folks sent them back and that's when my folks found out. They weren't mad or anything. Just surprised. They never knew I was writing any books but they'd heard about the poems and other stuff. Some of the other kids in class told on me to their folks and their folks told my folks, who wondered what I was up to. My folks were bothered a bit cause I might spend time reading and writing instead of doing my chores. So they'd ask me about it now and then. I'd always tell 'em I only write a little bit at night when everything is done. That's a lie sorta cause I'm always writing in my head but sometimes I have to memorize it and keep it there until I can get back to the house and write stuff down. Besides, I was just writing songs by then.

I got them three spiral notebooks I sent to the New York publisher back the same day as Russell Davidson's funeral. Which meant there was two big let-downs for me that same day.

Twenty-Four

After Russell's funeral it didn't rain a drop for two weeks and then about forty drops fell one day. August came and it still didn't rain. You could see the corn wasn't producing no ears and the leaves was gettin' brown. Same with soybeans. Tobacco just didn't grow and the weatherman on television kept complaining that his garden was suffering and people's lawns were turning brown. Then he'd say it was good news for the weekends cause you didn't have to worry about it raining on your plans. Well, we planned to have some good crops this year and we'd have been mighty thankful to have some rain fall on those plans.

Daddy was scared, I could see it in his face. He was short with me, too, and at home he'd just sit quiet and not say anything. Course he was a worrier anyway, frettin' about everything under the sun, whether he needed to or not, but this was serious and he had good reason to worry so he worried extra hard. Finally it come time to cut tobacco and our crop looked pitiful. I looked at that crop and all I could see was hard times. I didn't know how we was going to make it.

From about the middle of August until after Labor Day was tobacco cutting time. It was also the hottest time of the year when the sun beat down so hard the shade just got up and left. At least that's what Daddy always said. He said, "It's so hot the shade got up and left." Actually, that's not totally true. There was still shade but that shade stopped being cool in August.

During tobacco cutting time we'd always start real early in the morning. Me and Daddy'd get to the barns for the feeding and milking about six and then we'd load tobacco sticks on the cart and make sure the tobacco knives and the spears were sharp and everything was ready. I'd eat something when I first got up, then I'd always get a snack right before eight o'clock when we'd all start working in the tobacco fields. You'd have to wait that long so the dew would dry off the tobacco or else it might all rot when you put it in the barn.

The first thing you do is cut the tobacco down, two rows at a time. There's a lead row cutter and then the follow row. That means the first man cuts two rows and lays them to his right just under the row of standing tobacco. The next guy comes along, just a little behind him, and cuts his tobacco and lays it down on top of those rows, tossing the tobacco to his left. That means four rows of standing tobacco are in one lay row. That's what we call it, a lay row.

You go down your two rows cutting and then at the end move over and cut coming back. You have to keep your back bent and head down the whole time, push the leaves up on the tobacco with your left hand and swing that tobacco knife with your right. That's if you're right handed. If you are left-handed everything is backward. It's hard to cut tobacco if you're left handed and we only hired one left-handed man.

After the rows are cut then you take an armful of tobacco sticks, which are thin sticks about four feet long with one end pointed, and drop them along the row so there is one stick for every five or six plants of tobacco. Depends on how big the tobacco is; big plants you can only get five on a stick while smaller plants can fit six and sometimes in a wash or at the ends of the row you might get seven plants on a stick.

After the sticks are dropped you get your spear, which looks like a long sharp hollow metal cone and you put it on the end of a tobacco stick, bend over and pick up a plant of tobacco and put the end of the stalk on that spear. The plants have to be speared near the end of the stalk, in the fat part toward the bottom, but if you get too close to the end the stalk will split so then you have to turn the plant over on its other side and try to spear that and be more careful the next time.

That's hard work, reaching down for every plant and then raising up and spearing it and running it down the stick. Then getting the next one and next one until you get the stick full, then you walk over and lay it down flat on the ground and start a pile. Those piles have to be about twelve feet apart and are about three feet high to make loading them easier.

After a bunch of tobacco is speared on sticks and put in piles, somebody drives a tractor pulling a cart down the field between those piles of tobacco. You stop the cart, get off the tractor, and put those sticks of tobacco on the cart. You have to lay them special. You start at the back of the cart and put the first stick down with the butts sticking out just at the end of the cart, then the following stick of tobacco a little further in until you have about four and then you put the last stick facing the other way, pointing towards the tractor with the butts flush against that end of the cart. Then you add another one or two directly on top of that stick at the front of the cart and set others down on the cart until you get the last one and you put that one on the other way, with the butts pointing back and add one or two and start back again. That way you can get a lot of tobacco on a cart.

The one putting the tobacco on the cart has to count and you always want a hundred sticks of tobacco on the cart, then you drive that cart full of tobacco to the barn and back it under where you want it hung and unfasten the chain and dump that cart. Now there are some tricks to dumping a cart full of tobacco, like you always put straw on the cart before you start loading it so the tobacco will slide out easy and you always want the front end of the cart heavier than the back so it gives better balance. Once the cart goes up you have to let the clutch out of the tractor fast so the pile will slide off. If it doesn't slide then the whole pile of tobacco will drag forward. Also that jerk when you pop the clutch gets the tobacco going off the cart. You can rip tobacco up bad if you don't do it right.

A tobacco barn is filled with tier poles about four feet apart vertically and horizontally. The bottom tier poles are nailed down and are about eight feet off the ground. The low ground poles are about four feet off the ground but you keep them laying in a corner until you need them.

Somebody always has to hang the tobacco and that means climbing to the top of the barn and then somebody else is up in the barn too to hand it to him and another is on the ground to take it off the pile and pass it up. Then, when the top gets hung, the top guy drops down until the one passing it up in the barn isn't needed. You keep doing that until the barn is full of tobacco.

When I was young I drove the tractor while Daddy or Uncle Roadkill or somebody loaded the cart, but that was a luxury. Usually whoever loads the cart also drives the tractor and keeps count, too. If they lose count then somebody in the barn has to count the sticks.

The first real job for kids is cutting tobacco. Kids are smaller and it's not as hard on their back as it is on a grown man who has to bend over further, but grown men are usually more careful. Usually you don't want kids spearing tobacco at first cause they can run that spear clear through their hand. You have to be a little bigger, at least as big as a tobacco stick and that's four feet tall.

If you manage it right you can hire some local kids; there are always fathers around who've grown up on a farm and want their kids to have a taste of cutting tobacco. I don't know why. Share the experience, I guess. Figured they had to do it so their kids have to suffer too.

There's always local kids in town who want to do it to make some money, but some just can't take it. A lot of times you'll have a bunch of kids in the field at the start of tobacco cutting and by noon the first day a bunch of 'em have gone home, but the rule is you have to stay the whole day to get paid. That means a lot of 'em suffer until the end of that day and then you just don't see 'em in those tobacco fields any more.

I never had no choice, though. I have to be out there every day, day in and day out whether I like it or not. Besides, I can handle the work.

Cutting tobacco is the one time Daddy hires people to work. Cutting tobacco is just too hard and you have to get it done quick or else it will go to ruin so he hires some kids to cut and usually a couple of men—hired hands who do farm work whenever they can—and then a couple of colored. Pay is $8 a day for a top hand, $5 if he's colored. The boys get $3 a day.

Ideally, you want to manage your workers so everybody is always working and there ain't no idle time. First thing in the morning everybody cuts tobacco so you can get started but soon that's a boy's job and the men spear. Course the boys can't get too far ahead and so you have to get them to stop and do odd jobs, like get water for the men. Usually you just cut and spear all morning and then in the afternoon start hauling tobacco to the barn or maybe load up a cart just before dinner at noon so's a crew can start in the barn right after dinner.

Boy those tobacco cutting dinners are something. Twelve noon everybody heads to the house and washes up. There are always two pans and two buckets, one for the colored and one for the whites. Tobacco is covered with a black gum-like tar that gets all over you. You have to scrub that tobacco gum off pretty hard to get clean. Your clothes are all covered with that stuff, too. Some town boys are always surprised by this and quit right after they find that gum on them.

After washing up we wait until Mama gives the word and then we come inside for dinner. The whites all eat at the middle room table and the colored eat in the kitchen. If you only hire one colored he eats by himself but he always has exactly the same food we do, just in a different room. And boy that food is ripe for eatin'.

There'll always be a couple of different meats—usually beef and ham and then some mashed potatoes and green beans and peas and corn and squash. Lots of bowls all over the table filled up with food. Most everything comes right out of the garden. Big red ripe tomatoes. I love tomatoes when they drip. Biscuits made from scratch. Plenty of sweet iced tea and lots of time a slice of cake for desert. Yellow cake with chocolate icing. Talk about food fittin' to eat, that's it.

After you finish eating you go outside and kinda lay around a little bit and then head back to the fields. We have to be working again at one o'clock, which means there is a whole hour off for lunch. That's like paradise in the middle of the day. Before heading back out to the fields we always get jugs of water filled up again with ice in them. There is always a jug for the colored and one for the whites but Daddy and Uncle Roadkill each have their own jugs. That's cause we have spring water while Uncle Roadkill has artesian water. Once you drink a certain kind of water and get used to it any other kind won't satisfy your thirst. Like you get used to drinking spring water and then you try drinking artesian water and you'll drink and drink and drink and still be thirsty, but a good mouthful of spring water will do you fine.

It takes about three weeks of solid work to finish cutting tobacco. We finished on Labor Day and the day after that all us kids went back to school.

Twenty-Five

When school started in September of 1965 it was different because it was the first time I'd ever been to an integrated school. I don't know why they waited so long cause people was always talking about it. In fact, they had been talking about it for years and people was always scared it was gonna happen. Scared that all the white girls would get raped by big black guys and it wouldn't be safe for nobody. The logic was that the colored had their own schools and did alright and didn't want to be part of that mess anyway so what was all the fuss about? Why mess with a good thing that's working?

I'd gone to the same school all my life, eleven years, and didn't want to go to a new school for my last year but they didn't ask me and even if they did it wouldn't have made no never mind. They took two white high schools and one black school and put them all together into one big high school with grades nine through twelve. Before that everybody was in the same school, grades one through twelve, but now it got divided up.

That first day of school was scary. Twenty-six police cars in front of the school and police in riot gear walking around with helmets and billy clubs. Some carried a rifle. Parents standing out in the parking lot watching and I know for a fact a bunch of them had brought guns along in case something broke out. They was talking real loud amongst themselves and you could hear the word nigger a lot but nobody yelled anything directly at the kids.

The kids were all scared to death. Both black and white kids were scared. I remember feeling scared and I was white. I felt like I was in the middle of something that was going to explode and you didn't know where all the pieces were going to fly or how it was going to turn out but there wasn't nothing to do except hope you didn't die or get hurt bad. Otherwise you just kept going where the teachers and everybody pointed you to go. Like I said, I felt scared and I thought I was on the good side.

On that first day we all got off the buses and marched in to the schools and into our rooms and got assigned a seat. Sometimes you had to sit by a colored cause they put us all in alphabetical order but that wasn't a big deal to me. Tommy Senior Morgan was right upset and let it be known loud and clear that he wouldn't stand for his daughter sitting next to some nigger boy but that didn't happen. She sat between two other white girls. Got the luck of the draw, I reckon.

The whole first week of school was like that, with police in riot gear and parents in the parking lot, but then it kinda settled down and after that there was only a couple of police around and they wasn't wearing no riot gear. The kids' daddies mostly quit coming after that first week. There was just a couple of mama's out there in the parking lot.

By the third week everybody'd mostly gotten used to it. Not that everybody thought integration was any better or the answer to anything. Everybody still believed things were better the way they were before. At least that's what the folks I knew thought and said and that's what they told each other. After awhile, I guess people figured that this was the way it is now so you just get used to it and go on about your business. At least that's what I did.

I found out the colored weren't nearly as bad as everybody claimed and sometimes I'd catch a glimpse of one and he'd look just as scared as us white folks. Uncle Roadkill used to go on about there being a difference between niggers and colored and that he hated niggers but didn't mind colored. According to Roadkill, the colored were all right because they knew their place but the niggers just wanted to cause trouble. I told Uncle Roadkill that as far as I could see they was all colored going to our school. He said they was all niggers or else they wouldn't a been there.

The third weekend in September is the St. John's County Fair. That was always the social highlight of the year for me cause my 4-H projects got put on display. I also got a chance to win a bunch of money with prizes. Last year I won $121 in prize money. If that ain't the Big Time, I don't know what is. The biggest prize awarded at the Fair was $20 for Top Hog, and I got it. I also had a steer I showed—but only won third—and some tobacco, corn and hay. There was some other stuff too, like livestock judging. I even went to the State Fair last summer on the livestock judging team.

The one thing I didn't win was the tractor driving contest and that came with a big trophy. People was looking for me when that contest went on but I'd gone down to the carnival grounds just horsing around with some others. Didn't think I was going to enter it so I lost out there.

The most tragic thing that happened, and what embarrassed me the most, involved Clarissa Longley. Oh, my was she a looker. Only 15 but stacked to the max, as Willie Glaser said. He also said that she didn't have much upstairs, but boy she sure had a great staircase. Every boy in 4-H was after her, flirting and what-not, following her around like a whipped puppy. I wasn't no exception.

One afternoon I was wrestling with her in this big ole pile of straw when I looked up and lo and behold there was Daddy standing there watching us. I stopped and he says, "Does that steer have enough water?" I said "I'll check" and jumped right up and got a bucket and headed to the water spigot. Filled that bucket up to the brim and took it to the steer, who stuck his nose in and then pulled it out. That wasn't the last time I flirted with Clarissa but it was the last time I got caught by my Daddy. In fact, it was chasing after Clarissa that caused me to lose the tractor driving contest. All I could do was follow her around and as long as she was in my line of vision I lost sight of time and everything else. This was before Kathleen Holt entered my life.

Nothing ever came to anything with Clarissa. She had a way of flirting with you until you'd spent all your money on her at some fool carnival stand and won her a teddy bear or something and then she'd go on to some other guy and get him to spend his money. I won her a real nice teddy bear once and she named it "Wayne" after this other guy she had a fancy on. To top it all off, last year I bought her and me a candy apple. We was walking around eating them when a bee landed on mine that I didn't see and bit into. It stung my top lip and that lip swelled up so big I could hardly talk. Hung way out over the bottom one. Hurt too. Clarissa just kept saying "It must've been a girl bee." Well, I didn't even try to kiss her after that; if she'd a kissed back the pain would have driven me crazy.

This year the crops aren't too good what with the lack of rain and all but I had a good stick of tobacco and won third and my corn won fourth. My hogs did pretty good but I only won First prize for the pen of three, not Top Hog and the $20 first prize. My steer, which was an Angus—the first time I didn't have a Hereford—won fourth.

Twenty-Six

Actually, I was more excited about the Talent Contest this year, held on Friday night in the main building. Billy Boy Lindsley and I had been talking about the Fair's Talent Contest since we didn't get to play in the Fourth of July contest. We'd practiced every Saturday night all summer and there was no stopping us from getting in this Talent Contest. We was getting a lot better every week and both of us thought we'd be ready for a crowd when the Fair rolled around.

I'd learned to hear chord changes in songs from listening to the radio, then playing those songs. Country songs ain't usually that hard to figure out, although sometimes I had a hard time trying to figure out the key. I learned that there is an up chord and a down chord to a key. Like if you're in the key of C, then F is the up chord and G is the down chord. If you hear a song go up, go to the up chord, if it goes down, then go to the down chord. There's also what I call a passing chord. If you're in the key of C then the passing chord is D—or usually D seventh—and it usually comes in the bridge or chorus. Every key has a minor chord connected to it, too. For C that related chord is A minor.

You can take that idea of up and down chords and put them in any key. Like if you're playing in the key of D the up chord is G and the down chord is A. The passing chord is E seventh and the related minor is B minor. These things might not make sense to anybody else, but they work for me.

I also learned to hear the difference between a major and a seventh chord, or a major and a minor. A lot of times in country songs the down chord is a seventh and so is the passing chord. Keys give me the most trouble. First, I might sing the song in a key different from the song on the radio, so when I sat down to sing the song, naturally I went to my own key. Sometimes that meant the song wouldn't sound exactly like the version on the radio so I'd have to play along with the radio until I found the key.

The major keys aren't much of a problem—keys like A, C, D, E or G—but a lot of country songs are in keys like E flat or B flat or something like that. More songs than you would imagine are in those crazy keys. Those keys gave me fits until I found out about capos, which are things you put on the neck of a guitar so you can finger in a normal key but play in another key. Like you put that capo, which is a hard bar with an elastic piece that you wrap around your guitar neck so the top of the capo works like the end of the neck—on the third fret and you play in G fingering—that's G, C, and D with A seven your passing chord and E your minor—and it's actually in the key of B flat. Pretty tricky, but I caught on fast.

About a week before the Talent Contest Billy Boy said he'd talked to the guy in charge of the Talent Show and filled out a form and turned it in to get us in the contest. I told him I was glad he'd done that. I'd been wondering how to get into that contest without Daddy telling me it wasn't worth the time and Mama saying it might embarrass the whole family by me being up there and then going on about how I'd better practice ducking tomatoes and eggs while I sang just in case the crowd didn't like my singing.

I'd already told Mama and Daddy that the next Talent Contest I got in I wanted to sing with Billy Boy Lindsley and that if Charlene and the Pinworth girls wanted to sing, I'd play along with them too but Billy Boy came first. At first Mama said that my sister should be more important than Billy Boy but Charlene made it clear that she didn't ever want to enter a Talent Show again. She said going through that ordeal once was enough. Plus she and the Pinworth girls had a falling out when school started and they wasn't speaking to one another.

Soon as Billy Boy told me he'd sent in the form I told Mama and Daddy that me and Billy Boy was going to be in the St. John's County Fair Talent Contest. First thing Daddy said was that it wasn't worth the time to be in a Talent Show like that and then Mama said it might embarrass the whole family by me being up there and then she went on about how I'd better practice ducking tomatoes and eggs while I sang just in case the crowd didn't like my singing.

Me and Billy Boy started working on two songs for the contest. We also wanted to have one worked up for an encore because the top three winners always got to do another number. The first song we picked to do was the old Everly Brothers song, "Bye Bye Love." That's a good up tempo song and our voices blend good on it. We sing that whole song together and I've got the guitar part down good. Billy Boy comes in with a strong rhythm and has the lead vocal. For our second song we worked on "Wild Side of Life," which we both sang the whole way through. That is a slower song and it lets our harmonies really shine.

I wanted to do one of the songs I wrote but Mama always said nobody wants to hear something you made up. People want to hear what they know. That's exactly what she said, "Nobody wants to hear something you made up. People want to hear what they know." And Daddy kept saying I shouldn't take advantage of a crowd gathered to hear talent by inflicting them with something of my own like some fool song I'd written. In fact, he insisted that the crowd came and paid good money to hear some talent and I was wasting their time and money to even be up there on the stage. If that was true, then a lot of other talent had wasted my time and money through the years. I'd stood there and took it for years and didn't mind too much. Goes with the territory. Go to a talent show and hope you hear somebody talented. It ain't no sure bet, but then again, that's what makes it interesting, especially when somebody really bombs. I've seen people up there so bad that I got embarrassed for them, and I was sitting out in the audience.

Billy Boy didn't want us to do one of my songs either. He said it might confuse the judges too much if we played something nobody'd heard before. He'd been writing some songs too but he didn't think any of his was good enough yet. He thought some of mine might be good enough but he wasn't sure the judges would have the sense to realize it. He wanted to play it safe with songs everybody knew so we did.

For our encore song we planned on doing an old Wilburn Brothers song, "Trouble's Back in Town." The Wilburn Brothers have good high lonesome harmonies and me and Billy Boy had their sound down pat. We felt pretty good with those three songs and even felt we had a shot at winning.

Both me and Billy Boy knew this was the big time but we thought we could handle it. Billy Boy practiced his autograph a lot but I never did that. Figured I knew my own name good enough to write it down if somebody asked. I just couldn't imagine anybody'd ask, so that was a waste of time. Billy Boy said you never know what's gonna happen so it's better to be prepared. He prepared himself for signing autographs real good.

We did talk about outfits and decided on dark dress pants—his were black and mine was Navy blue—a white shirt and then those western ties that have a bow at the top and two ribbons hanging down. I thought we looked pretty sharp myself but Mama kept after me to polish my shoes. I told her nobody looked at shoes. I know I didn't ever notice what kind of shoes somebody else was wearing. She said what about Aunt Tootie and Aunt Noodles and people like that. I must admit they noticed everything so before I left the house for the Talent Show I took a wet rag and wiped off my shoes.

The Talent Show had 15 acts on it and Billy Boy and I was seventh. They put everybody's name in a hat and drew out numbers, which is how come we ended up where we did. We called ourselves The Double D Boys. We was going to use the stage names of Duane and Daryl, but nothing ever came of it. Besides, we wouldn't a fooled nobody in that audience cause they knew who we really was anyway.

I felt like this was a big break we was about to get and that we was headed for a career in show business and I was ready to work hard at it, to put my whole self into this performance. That made me feel nervous but excited, too. I was scared we'd mess up but I was rarin' to get up and give it a shot. By the time the show started, I just wanted to get up there and get it over with but we had to wait for six acts to do their thing before we had our shot.

The act right before us was seven grown women singing barbershop harmonies and right after us was four grown men in a barbershop quartet. The first act was a ten year old kid trying to tell jokes and the second was a girl who tap danced, so that gives you an idea of how the whole thing started off, but it was rolling along pretty good by the time me and Billy Boy got on stage.

Our first song, "Bye, Bye Love" went over pretty good but it was mostly a young crowd, people our age, and they didn't care much for country music or old Everly Brothers songs. So the idea of doing "Wild Side of Life" wasn't as appealing when we finished "Bye Bye Love" as it had been when we was rehearsing. There were some guys tanked up yelling "rock'n'roll" so me and Billy Boy suddenly got hit with the dumb ass standing right there on stage and decided to do "Can't Buy Me Love" by the Beatles, which we'd only sorta practiced twice. Actually, we did it in Billy Boy's bedroom just killing time and clowning around but we did it that night with him and me both singing lead together cause we'd never worked out any harmony parts or anything. Both of us missed a chord here and there but we both finished together. So that was that and there wasn't no opportunity for "Trouble's Back in Town" or any other song for that matter.

The women who sang right before us won third prize—which is as high as the prizes went. Second prize went to a band, The Surfers, who did "Wooly Bully" and it was pretty good. But the Grand Prize winner was the Wanderers. What they did knocked the socks off everybody.

The Wanderers are the top band in our area. They play at all the school dances and stuff. They did "Pretty Woman" and they did it exactly like the Roy Orbison record, that was how good they was. Lick for lick and word for word. They came out with funny looking paint on their lips and hands and about half-way through their song somebody hit the lights and the place went total dark except for some black lights at the front of the stage. The lead singers lips were painted with that paint that glows with a black light so you could see them moving when he sang. The guitar player's fingers and the drummer's hands was also painted and the guitars and drum sticks were outlined with that special paint. I mean to tell you it was the most incredible, exciting thing that'd ever happened in a Talent Show at the St. John's County Fair in the history of mankind. Naturally, they took the big prize and then played at the dance afterward.

By that time there was plenty of people tanked up pretty good so we only stayed around a little while. There was going to be some fights and maybe some shooting and I didn't feel like putting up with that. People walking up to you, slugging you in the shoulder or arm and then daring you to fight and they've got all their buddies with them and a knife or gun in their pocket and they picked you cause you were alone. No siree, I'd been through that before.

What I hadn't figured on was being a celebrity. Lots of people came up to me and Billy Boy and said "nice job" or "I didn't know you was that good." That was always the highest compliment cause everybody around me always told me I wasn't worth a flip. And three junior high girls asked me and Billy Boy for our autographs. So we felt pretty good afterwards, even though we lost.

Mama and Daddy didn't come and watch us. Mama said something about being scared she'd have an earache when we finished and Daddy said we'd only make fools of ourselves and we could do that on our own. Mama also said she'd just wait and watch us when we got on television and Daddy said he didn't want to fight the traffic and crowd to set with a bunch of sweaty drunks. I wanted them to see me and Billy Boy play cause I wanted them to know how good we was but I understood their point of view—they just wasn't used to having somebody they know on a stage in front of a lot of people and they weren't exactly sure how to act.

That Talent Show didn't make me and Billy Boy big stars but it was another important step in show biz and we learned a real valuable lesson: we both vowed never again to try and play a song we hardly knew for a whole crowd of people, even if somebody requested it.

*T*wenty-*S*even

Our telephone hung on the kitchen wall so's Mama could work in the kitchen and talk at the same time. We had got that telephone right after I started the ninth grade. One night after the St. John's County Fair's Talent Show while we was eating supper it rang. Actually, it rang fairly often what with Aunt Tootie and Aunt Noodles burning up those phone lines on this that or t'other, and every now and then somebody called Daddy. But this night it rang for me.

We was surprised it rang during supper cause usually nobody called during that time. The people who usually called us ate supper about the same time as we did but Mama got up from the table and answered it, then she looked at me and just sorta held the phone in my direction and I got up and took it and said "Hello" like you're supposed to do.

"Compton? This is Shock O'Connell."

"Oh, hi, Mr. O'Connell." I have known Shock O'Connell my whole life I reckon—or rather I've known who he is—but we'd never spoken to each other. He was the grown-up who owned an electricity company that wired people's houses and fixed plugs and stuff like that. His real name was J. Benjamin O'Connell, which was painted on the side of his trucks and Billy Boy Lindsley's Daddy worked for him. Course, Billy Boy worked for him too ever since he'd graduated.

"Compton, you can forget that Mr. stuff, y'hear? You call me Shock cause that's what everybody else calls me."

"Yes, sir, Mr. Shock," I said. Then I caught myself and said, "I mean Shock."

"That's better, much better. Compton, how's it been going for you?" I said, "O.K. Pretty good, I guess."

"Well, that's good. Good to hear that. Well, we've had a long, dry summer."

"Yes sir, we have," I said. Then I paused a bit before he said, "You been pickin' that guitar much lately?"

"Oh, yes, sir," I said. "I pick something most every day. Might not be too much but every single day I sit down with that guitar and play some songs."

"Well, that's great, Compton, but you cut that 'Sir' stuff out. I'm just Shock."

"Oh, yes, sir. I mean yes. I forgot."

He chuckled. "Well, that's alright. You know Garner's been pickin' some too. He's learnin' the steel guitar. And I pick some myself." That was the first I ever knew of that. His son, Garner, was a year ahead of me in school, in the same class with Billy Boy.

Then he said "I was hopin' maybe that we might get together sometime and pick."

I jumped on that pretty quick and said, "Oh, yeah, that would be great. I love to pick guitar."

"Yea, I've heard you do. And I know you're pretty good. What are you doing tonight?"

I told him I was eating supper and then he asked if I'd like to come over to his house after I finished my supper and I said "Yes, I reckon so. I mean I sure would but I need to check with my folks."

And he said "Good, good. Well, then, I'll see you in a little while. Billy Boy Lindsley is coming over, too. I just talked to him. You might want to call and see if you can catch a ride over together."

"That's great," I said. "I'll do that."

"All right," he said. "I'll see you guys in a little while." And then he hung up.

Back at the supper table I was all pumped up and told everybody "That was Shock O'Connell and he wants me to come over to his house and pick some on the guitar" and then asked if that was all right. Mama said she had gone to school with Shock's sister-in-law and that Shock's grandfather was the biggest rascal ever known in these parts. Daddy said it didn't make no difference, wasn't nothing gonna come out of it anyway except I'd embarrass myself, so go on with my foolishness and get it out of my system. That's exactly what he said, "Go on with your foolishness and get it out of your system."

Just then the phone rang again and I jumped up to answer it. It was Billy Boy.

"Did Shock call you?" he asked.

"Sure did," I said. "He wants us to come over to his house and pick some. You going?"

"You bet," he said. "How about you?"

"Yep, I sure am. Can you swing by and give me a ride?"

"No problem," he said. "I'll see you in a few minutes." And then he hung up.

Well I couldn't eat fast enough and then I got my guitar and got to the front door just as I saw Billy Boy's headlights coming down the road. "I've got a ride with Billy Boy," I said. "So I don't need to use the car."

"Well, that's good," said Daddy. "Cause I'd have to think about you using it. What time you gonna be home?"

"I don't know," I said. "We're going to pick awhile."

Then Mama said, "Catnap, are you sure we should let Compton ride over with Billy Boy?"

"Billy Boy's a good driver," I said quickly. "He drives real safe."

Mama looked hard at Daddy, who was looking down at his plate as he sopped up the last pieces of food with his piece of bread. Then he said, "Shock O'Connell just wired those new houses that Jim Snyder built just outside of Lynnville."

I wasn't sure what that meant cause Mama was still staring at him while he was looking down at his plate but I didn't wait around to find out. I bolted out the door and jumped in Billy Boy's car and we took off for Shock O'Connell's house.

"Shock O'Connell said him and Garner both play," I said to Billy Boy soon as I got in his car. "I didn't know that. Did you?"

"Well, sorta. Daddy said Shock likes country music and likes to mess around with it. And Daddy's said he's heard him play the steel guitar. It's set up down in the basement."

"Have you ever been over there before?" I asked.

"Oh, yea, of course" he said. "I work there, remember? But I've just been outside at the warehouse behind his house. That's where the trucks and electrical stuff are kept. I've never been inside the house."

"Well, looks like we might see the inside tonight," I said.

"Yep, sure will," was all he said.

We pulled up into the O'Connell's driveway and knocked on the side door. That's the one Billy Boy said they all used. Mrs. O'Connell called out "Come in" and when we did she said "They're all in the basement. Go right on down" and she pointed to an open door with some stairs leading down.

Shock O'Connell had a little stage set up in his basement that was on the left at the bottom of the steps. Straight ahead was a pool table. There was a bunch of amps and microphones and even a drum set on that stage. Ardmore Pinworth, brother to the Pinworth girls, was on the drum set and Garner O'Connell was playing a guitar. Shock O'Connell was playing the steel guitar. Soon as we walked in they all told us to sit down, pull out our guitars and play a few songs with them.

Well, me and Billy Boy took out our guitars, got them tuned up with everybody else's, then we kicked off with "Fraulein" with Billy Boy singing lead and me singing on the chorus. Next we did "Hey, Good Lookin" and Billy Boy sang lead on that one too with me doing harmony all the way through. Then I sang "Pick Me Up On Your Way Down" and everybody jumped in and played along and liked it while Billy Boy added some harmony on the chorus.

We did that for a couple of hours—somebody would call out a song and we'd find a key and play it. I knew the words to a lot of songs so I sung a bunch of them. Billy Boy knew a lot of words but couldn't play as good so sometimes he'd just sing and not play and I'd sing harmony with him. We done that until after nine o'clock that night—we'd gotten there about 6:30—and I thought I'd died and gone to heaven. I'd been playing songs by myself or with Billy Boy so long and I was just glad to be picking with other people.

Right after nine we took a break and Shock started talking about us being a band and working up some songs and all and practicing regular. We all liked that idea just fine. Especially me and Billy Boy cause we'd been tossing around the idea of putting together a band for a while but hadn't really done anything about it. Then Shock said, "We're going to need electric guitars if we're going to play out."

Well, my heart just about sunk cause all I had was my Silvertone flat-top and I just flat out couldn't afford no electric. Shock must've noticed my face cause then he said, "You pick good, Compton. You're a good take-off guitar player. How about if I lend you the money to buy a guitar and you can pay me back later?"

"I don't know how I could pay you back" was all I could think of so that's what I said.

"You can pay me back from money we get playing out," he said. That was the first time I ever thought about actually getting money to play music like it was a job. I'd thought about winning something in a talent contest—sometimes they have a cash prize—but I'd never thought about making money playing. So I said all right and then he made the same deal with Billy Boy and offered to sell Ardmore the drum set on the same kind of arrangement. By that time Mrs. O'Connell had brought down some soft drinks and chips. After we finished our drinks, Billy Boy took me home.

I was sure excited so when I got home I told Mama and Daddy about Shock lending me the money for an electric guitar so we could have a band. The first thing Daddy said was "You dream up some foolishness and you're in debt already" and Mama said "Why don't you play and get the money first and then buy the guitar."

Well, I tried to explain that you can't play on a bandstand without an electric guitar cause you won't be heard and Mama just said "It might be better if they didn't hear you anyway" and Daddy chimed in "If they heard you play they might want their money back." So I just give up and went to bed, but I was bound and determined to get me an electric guitar.

On Saturday morning Billy Boy picked me up and we all met over at Shock O'Connell's house again, like we'd agreed to do, and went down to a music store in Boscoe, about 25 miles away. There was a whole bunch of guitars hanging on the walls. Billy Boy got his guitar first—it was a used Silvertone electric and it felt pretty good. It was only about $100, which was a ton of money. I would never have even thought about spending that much money on a guitar until we got into that store and I found out real quick that electric guitars can cost you a pretty bundle. So I changed my way of thinking and started thinking that a hundred dollars wasn't really that much money. Course, I wasn't thinking about paying it back right then; I was just thinking about spending it.

I found me a used Gretsch guitar and it was a beaut—just like Chet Atkins had on the cover of one of his record albums. I had that record. I'd seen pictures of George Harrison of the Beatles playing that same guitar too. It was $300 but Shock O'Connell paid out the money without batting an eye and said "You'll make that much and then some once we get going." I liked hearing about myself getting rich and decided it would be an easy adjustment for me to make.

Usually on a Saturday I've got to work on the farm but this Saturday it was raining so there wasn't much we could do so the band all went back to Shock O'Connell's house, plugged in and started playing. This time Shock didn't play much but he had Garner switch to steel guitar. Garner wasn't as good as his Daddy but he was all right and he was learning quick. I started working on lead runs and over that rainy afternoon I just fell in love with my guitar. It was maroon red.

Wouldn't you know we played all afternoon—until 5:30—and my fingers were sore but I wasn't feeling a bit tired. I didn't think it was even possible for me to ever get tired playing music. At the end of that day we had a list of twenty-two songs that we felt pretty comfortable with. Then I went home and did the feeding and had supper.

I was so full of happy I was ready to bust at supper. I started telling Daddy and Mama and them about all that was going on but Mama she just couldn't get over me spending that much money on a guitar. Money that I didn't have. And Daddy said I'd drive us all to the poor house spending money like that. I thought we was already in the poor house so I didn't see what big difference one guitar would make.

Mama said I'd better learn how to save money before I learned how to spend it. That's exactly what she said, "Compton, you'd better learn how to save money before you learn how to spend it." Daddy said the racket I was raising with my regular guitar was bad enough and that now things would be even worse cause I'd be even louder and then Mama jumped in and said at least this guitar had a button you could turn down. That's when Daddy asked, "Can you turn it off." I said "yes" and Daddy said that guitar might be an answer to prayer.

I told them I bought the same guitar Chet Atkins was holding on one of his album covers. I even went and got the album and showed it to them. Mama said "If Chet Atkins ever finds out you bought a guitar just like him he'll probably get rid of his." Daddy said I'd better be careful getting too uppity and thinking I was better than I really was and that I wasn't no Chet Atkins and I'd better not ever start thinking I was. That was exactly what he said to me, "You ain't no Chet Atkins so don't ever start thinking you are." Then Mama started asking about the amplifiers, which I'd been talking about. We was using Shock O'Connell's and I told her that. She said it didn't make no sense to own a guitar you couldn't play without electricity. What if the current went out? That's exactly what she said to me, "It don't make no sense to own a guitar you can't play without electricity. What if the current goes out?"

Mama said that the whole thing sounded like a plot to sucker you to spend money cause you couldn't just get a guitar any more, you had to have an amplifier too, and then if you don't pay your electric bill neither one would be any good. That's exactly what she said, "If you don't pay your electric bill neither that guitar or amplifier is going to do you any good."

I did my best to explain and showed them the new electric guitar. Daddy wanted me to plug it into the wall socket. I tried to explain that you can't just plug a guitar straight into a wall socket. Daddy said, "Then why do they call it an electric guitar? And what good is it if you can't plug it in a regular wall socket?" Mama kept saying that if it was electric it would drive up our electric bill and then we couldn't afford to pay it and we'd be in a world of hurt. That happened last winter with an electric heater they bought. They cranked that heater up for a month and then the feathers hit the tar paper when that electric bill came. Daddy said I'd just bought three or four ways to go broke when I bought that electric guitar. That's exactly what he said, "You've just bought three or four ways to go broke when you bought that electric guitar." The only thing Charlene said was "If you have an electric guitar, does that mean you'll quit playing that country music and start playing something decent for a change?" She must've asked me that forty-eleven times. I told her "no" every time.

After supper I went in my room and played my new maroon red electric guitar until it was time to go to bed. I practiced different runs on the neck. I thought about writing Chet Atkins a letter telling him about my guitar and asking if there was any tips I should know about playing it, but I didn't have his address.

Twenty-Eight

After that Saturday we practiced again on Sunday afternoon, then Tuesday night, Thursday night, Friday night and then Saturday night. On the following Tuesday night we all went over to Shock O'Connell's house to practice again. Shock made us play the same songs over and over and over again. We knew twenty-two songs real good.

That night we practiced our first three numbers and then Shock told us the big news: we had a gig that Friday night at Gilmore's Tavern and Bar. Well, the practice went a whole lot better after that. For outfits we decided we'd wear black and white. We all had white shirts, white sox, and black shoes, and Shock's wife went out and bought us each a black string tie, a black vest trimmed in white and black pants. We looked cool. And real sharp.

Friday night we met at Shock's house at six o'clock, loaded up the car with the equipment and set out to Gilmore's, which was about 17 miles away.

Gilmore's was down by the water, looking out over a little bay, and people came in to eat some food, drink and dance. There was a pool table in the middle of the room that we moved off to the side, then we set up in a corner.

Ardmore put his drum set right in the corner, then Garner put his steel guitar to Ardmore's right and just in front of him. Me and Billy Boy were right in front of Ardmore and we each of us had a microphone. We put all our amplifiers in a row in front of us. Shock said that let the customers hear the music better. The only problem was that it was hard for us to hear ourselves.

The first song we did was "Walk On By" by Leroy Van Dyke with that killer kick off guitar lick that I had down pat. Billy Boy sung lead and I came in on harmony on the chorus. Then we did "Waitin' in Your Welfare Line" and Billy Boy sang lead on that too while I did the take-off guitar runs after each line, then I stepped up and sang "Welcome To My World," a Jim Reeves ballad. By that time folks had started to get up and dance.

That line-up of those three songs never changed; they were always our first three songs. We played 'em one right after the other without a break cause when we kicked off a show we wanted to kick it off good. After those first three songs, we got into a lot of arguments about what to play next but those first three songs was always solid.

That first night we run out of songs pretty quick and started playing the ones we knew over again. Then people stated requesting songs and if me or Billy Boy knew the words we'd give it a shot. It might work and then again it might not. Sometimes we didn't know the words and the person who requested it would say "Let me sing it" so we'd try to find their key and let 'em. There was some pretty pitiful singing that night but everybody that sang had a good time and enjoyed hearing themself. Even if the other folks in the place weren't always too well pleased with the sound. Shock O'Connell grabbed the microphone about every half hour and said, "Drink up cause the more you drink the better these boys sound." He also said, "If you don't like the way these boys play, drink some more and they'll sound a whole lot better."

We weren't supposed to make any money that first night. Shock had told Bugs Gilmore to let us play for free and if he didn't like us then he didn't have to pay us or ask us back. Bugs agreed but some people brought some money up to us as tips and we collected $20 that way and then at the end of the night Bugs said he liked us so much that he gave us $32 wadded up in a roll. That was $8 each. It sure beat working for a living. A top hand in the tobacco field only got $8 a day, so I knew right there and then that here is where my future lay.

On the first night at Gilmore's we also learned a secret about saving our guitars in a fight. See, there'd always be a fight break out whenever we played. Usually they were small affairs with just a couple of guys involved but that first night there was a total free-for-all. Bugs had a baseball bat under his bar and he pulled it out and started swinging and heads started rolling. We managed to get into the bathroom with our guitars and lock the door. Actually, this is the embarrassing part because the first time a fight happened was around eleven at night and we got in the bathroom all right but the last time it was around one in the morning and the men's door was locked so we had to go into the women's room and lock the door, then some women came screaming and banging on the door but our guitars were valuable so we didn't let 'em in. Besides, it was embarrassing to be in there.

After the gig was over it felt like we was floating on Cloud Nine. We'd made $13 each for doing what we would've done for free. Now, you can't beat that in terms of making money. It was almost like stealing candy from a baby. We'd get up there and pick and sing and people would just throw money at us. I pictured myself doing this my entire life. All the way home in the car we was making big plans about stage outfits and new guitars and new microphones and playing whole weekends instead of just a Friday night.

All the band members was older than me. Billy Boy was one grade ahead of me at school but he was two years older cause he had been held back in the third grade. Nobody except the kids ever said "failed" at school. The grown-ups always said "held back." He was almost exactly the same size as me and we were built kinda alike, tall and skinny. He smiled a lot and liked to joke around. His hair was brown and went every which-a-way on his head.

Since last June, me and Billy Boy had gotten real close from our singing. When we sang together, with me doing the harmony to his lead vocal, it felt like we was one person. And we had started dreaming together, too. Both of us wanted to be in a band that played country music and both of us believed we had a future in music. That's mostly what we talked about—music. Me and Billy Boy would talk guitars or songs or singing for hours. We'd work out harmonies and I'd work out a lead part on guitar while he played rhythm. By the time we got to Shock O'Connell's house, we was real tight together. Almost to the point that each of us knew what the other would do when we was singing and playing together.

Billy Boy was pretty easy-going but Garner was a ball of fire. He was short—only five foot six—even though he'd graduated from high school two years before. He was all right once you got to know him but if you didn't know him he was liable to get in a fight with you. He smoked a lot, one cigarette after the other, and sometimes he'd laugh, but he wasn't the kind of person you could kid around with much. Now Billy Boy you could tease and carry on with, but Garner took things real serious, especially himself.

Ardmore Pinworth was our dandy. He was handsome and three years older than me and always had girls in love with him. I didn't mind him being so handsome except that he thought he was even more handsome than he actually was. Aunt Tootie used to say that Ardmore had a high opinion of himself and that no amount of compliments from other people could ever satisfy him so he had to keep telling himself he was wonderful. Ardmore had dark wavy hair that he combed every few minutes.

If a mirror was anywhere around, Ardmore couldn't look anybody but himself in the eye. I never saw anybody primp and preen more than he did, except his sisters. He spent more money on clothes than most girls did and he always smelled like after shave. He walked around like he was admiring himself. Aunt Noodles used to say that if everybody admired Ardmore as much as he admired himself there'd be statues of him all over the county. I liked Ardmore alright but, as Mama said, a little bit of Ardmore Pinworth goes a long ways.

Shock O'Connell was short too and he was 44 years old. He had thick wavy hair in front and a bald hole in the back. He had a belly that hung way out over his belt and he walked kinda bow-legged. Always had a cigar in his mouth, but sometimes it wasn't lit. Most of the time he had a can of beer in his hand, too. A lot of times he'd sip a long time on one can.

Shock always wanted to be in country music. Since he never made it he just lived the life as best he could. He owned tons of country records and a bunch of guitars. He was pretty good on the steel guitar and he'd always sit in on a song or two every night but he'd decided Garner would play steel and he'd be our manager. One of the things a manager needed to do, according to Shock, was name the band so he named us the Golden Melody Boys, but most of the time everybody just called us Shock O'Connell's band.

It was funny how we got our regular stage costumes. We started out wearing black and white and we all thought that was the cat's meow. We even went out and bought some black cowboy hats after we played that first night at Gilmore's but on the second Friday night we stopped at a five and dime on the way there cause Shock had to get something or other. At the front of the store was a table loaded with clothes with a sign that said "Everything Here 10 cents." On that table was four shirts that were shiny bright gold and it was an absolute miracle that they were the exact right sizes for all of us in the band so we bought those shirts and wore them when we played.

The first time we wore them was that night after our eleven o'clock break. We wore our regular black and white to start with. After we finished at Gilmore's that night I wore that shirt home. Next morning I brought it out and showed it to Mama and Daddy and said "Guess how much I paid for this?" Daddy looked at it and said, "Well, if you paid a quarter you paid too much." So I up and said, "Then I got a good deal I guess, cause I only paid a dime." I was smiling full of myself when I said it. Then Mama said, "If you paid a dime for that I hope they gave you a nickel change" and I said, "No, I was ready to give 'em even more money cause it's worth a whole lot more than ten cents." Daddy said "Well, don't look at a gift horse's mouth" and then he said "They ought to put those shirts in a horse's mouth." Then Mama she up and said real quick, "That would be the wrong end to put 'em in."

I could'a killed Charlene. She laughed her head off when Mama said that. Then she said, "Compton, it's bad enough being born ugly. You guys have to top it off by wearing ugly every time you play." Charlene might'a thought she had taste in clothes cause she talked about 'em all the time but she didn't really know clothes like she thought she did. It's true that a lot of people teased us about those shirts but I always knew that those shirts wasn't ugly.

Twenty-Nine

Our band got pretty well known pretty quick and we even got some followers who came to wherever we played. Course the girls all followed after Ardmore and he was serious with a different one each week. Aunt Tootie said Ardmore would never get married cause he could never find a girl who'd love him as much as he loved himself. It was hard to talk to Ardmore if you wasn't female and I wasn't. He wanted to sing "Danny Boy" about ten times a night. That was the main number he sang and we'd let him do it a couple of times. His other song was "Shenandoah." Course, when some girl came around he wanted to impress he'd bug us to death to do "Danny Boy." He sung it pretty good.

Billy Boy always had some girl flirting with him but Garner had a steady girl who was real quiet and she always came along. I didn't have many girls falling over me. Mostly, I had guys hanging around the bandstand trying to watch my fingers when I played and trying to talk about music on the breaks, which suited me just fine. I love music and I'd rather talk about that than anything. Besides, I carried the torch for Kathleen Holt.

Lots of times some guy would ask me to show him how to play a certain song or a certain take-off guitar run. Especially the Johnny Cash stuff. I had that boom-chicka-boom down pat, sounded just like ole Johnny's records. I'd muffle them strings with the heel of my hand to kill the vibration at just the right time and I could play the lead run on "Tennessee Flat-top Box" just like the record. Guys always wanted to know how to do that.

We set up regular practices every Tuesday and Thursday nights. Right after the first gig at Gilmore's The Golden Melody Boys got serious in a hurry about learning new songs. I'd work up three or four at home and so would Billy Boy and then we'd get together at practice and work on 'em as a band. We was pretty good. We'd run through a song a couple of times and we'd have it, then we'd always remember some song we'd tried on Friday night or something some drunk sang and we'd try to do it right.

The vocals were never a problem for me and Billy Boy. He sang lead on most of the songs and I had the harmony part. Soon as he started singing a song my harmony part fell in with him naturally and our voices blended good together. In about two months we knew over 200 songs, although I must freely and openly admit that we done some of them a whole lot better than we did others.

It was the fall of 1965 and we knew all the hot songs. Buck Owens was real big and we did his songs like "Together Again," "My Heart Skips a Beat," "I Don't Care," "I've Got a Tiger By the Tail," "Only You," "Act Naturally," "Love's Gonna Live Here," and "Above and Beyond." People couldn't hardly get enough of Buck Owens.

We also did "Saginaw, Michigan," "B.J. the D.J.," "Once a Day," "King of the Road," "Girl on the Billboard," "What's He Doing in My World," "She Thinks I Still Care," "Don't Let Me Cross Over," "Wolverton Mountain," "Talk Back Trembling Lips," and we even did "The Ballad of Jed Clampett" cause "The Beverly Hillbillies" was the best show on television. We'd do some oldies like "Oh Lonesome Me," "Release Me," "Blue Blue Day," "Billy Bayou," "White Lightning," "The Battle of New Orleans," "Please Help Me, I'm Falling," "He'll Have to Go," "Hello Walls," "My Special Angel," "Fraulein," "Singing the Blues," "I Walk the Line," "Blue Suede Shoes," "Folsom Prison Blues," "Tennessee Flat-top Box," "If You've Got the Money, I've Got the Time," and "Always Late."

The best songs for me and Billy Boy were the brother duets, like the Everly Brothers, or Louvin Brothers or Wilburn Brothers or Delmore Brothers. We did "Bye Bye Love," "Wake Up Little Susie," "All I Have to Do Is Dream," "Let It Be Me," "Blues Stay Away From Me," "Trouble's Back in Town," "When I Stop Dreaming," "I Take the

Chance" and "Must You Throw Dirt in My Face." Those brother duet songs were my favorite and me and Billy Boy did 'em just like the records.

And, Lawd Lawd did we do Hank Williams songs. In the first part of the evening people wanted to hear Buck Owens and the newer stuff, but as soon as they got a few beers in them, all they wanted to hear was Hank Williams. So we played songs like "Jambalya," "Cold Cold Heart," "Your Cheatin' Heart," "Hey Good Lookin'," "Why Don't You Love Me," "Kaw-Liga," "You Win Again," "I Can't Help It," "I'm So Lonesome I Could Cry," and I don't know what-all. If it was a Hank Williams song you can bet we did it sometime or other. If we didn't know it the person who requested it would sing it, which led to a lot of drunks falling all over our equipment.

Actually, letting drunks sing became a regular part of our show. See, when we started at Gilmore's we only knew twenty-two songs and that can't get you through six hours of playing a night. That's how long we played—six hours. Started at eight and went till two in the morning. Of course, we didn't play straight though. We got a break every two hours so at ten and midnight we took off for about 15 minutes.

After we played a couple a times at Gilmore's we started getting phone calls to play dances. We'd play at Gilmore's on Friday and then there'd be some dance on Saturday night. In October on the weekend when the time changed we played at Gilmore's on Friday night and then at Hank's Hideaway, which was a bar with a big dance floor, on Saturday night. We had a packed crowd and we was going good but I was gettin' tired cause I'd had to pick corn all Saturday before we played. I was having a good time but I was sure ready to quit when 2 a.m. rolled around.

Well, wouldn't you know it. It was the highlight of their lives for the folks at Hank's Hideaway to turn the hands of that clock back an hour as soon as it hit 2 a.m. so's they could get in an extra hour of drinking and partying. We didn't get paid any extra for it cause they said it was actually only one a.m. We had agreed to play to two so we done it but that was the longest hour of playing music I ever remember.

One weekend just before Christmas we played at Gilmore's, then at a wedding reception on Saturday afternoon, a dance Saturday night, and then on Sunday afternoon there was a special reception for somebody's anniversary. I felt pretty saturated with music that weekend but I must confess that the playing we did on Sunday afternoon definitely felt like a real job. By that time my voice was sore and so was my fingers. Somewhere along the line it had stopped being fun for just a little while and turned into work. We made a ton of money that weekend—each of the band members took home $150 when all was said and done. I felt like a man could make himself a good living, even support a family with that kind of money pouring in, but we never played that many different places in one weekend again.

Thirty

School settled into a pretty straight routine. I'd get up in the morning about 5 o'clock and feed the animals and milk Ole Brownie, who always gave more milk than any of our other cows. Daddy would milk two other cows in the time it was taking me to milk Brownie. Then I'd get back home, wash up and get something to eat and hightail it to Wendell's Store for the bus. It was an hour on that school bus every morning and every afternoon and that made me more tired than working.

I'd catch the bus at 7 in the morning and get to school by 8:15, which is when classes started, and then school let out at 3:15, which meant I got home about 4:30. Soon as I got home I'd change clothes and head to the barns and help Daddy with whatever. At 6 I'd do the night feeding, milk Brownie, and get back to the house around 6:45, have dinner and then start on my homework. It was my last year in school and I wanted to do a lot of things like work on the school paper or yearbook and play ball but I just couldn't. That farm took all my time and Daddy needed me too much. Plus, I was playing music now so Tuesday and Thursday evenings at 7 I went over to Shock O'Connell's and the nights at home I made sure I picked up the guitar and ran through a song or two on my own.

A lot of times I just felt wore out but most of the time I didn't mind this schedule all that much. Fall always means corn picking time and boy I loved that. I'd get home and change my clothes and run out to the field where Daddy was driving the corn picker. I'd get in the wagon hooked to the back of the corn picker and shuck the corn the picker didn't shuck. That was hard cause the corn kept dropping in the wagon. You'd reach for an ear of corn to shuck and then another ear would come right down on your hand or hit you somewhere else.

When the weather was right there would be a little coolness in the air and you could look up to the woods and see all kinds of colors and then maybe look overhead and see some geese flying in a "V." I always loved those beautiful October days riding in a wagon behind the corn picker but this year the corn ears weren't much to talk about. The dry weather had just about killed our corn crop and it didn't look like we'd have enough to feed the hogs for the coming year, much less have corn to sell for some extra money.

Combining soy beans was harder cause you sat out in the field on a wagon and waited until the grain tank of the combine filled up, then you'd drive over to the combine, pull up beside it and let the tank empty into burlap bags. There was an auger that come out and you'd hold a bag under that chute while somebody lifted a little lever to turn on the auger. When that bag was full you'd stop, pull the bag back, tie it up and grab another one. When the wagon was full of bags you'd take it to the barn and unload it. Stack up the bags of grain for winter feed.

Every single night I practiced my guitar some, even if it meant just making a few runs or strumming one song and singing it. Sometimes I'd be so tired I could hardly hold my head up, but I never let a single night go by without playing some music.

After our band got that job on Friday nights at Gilmore's I'd have to come home on Fridays, get the farm work done and then get over to Shock O'Connell's by around seven. We'd drive to Gilmore's, set up and start playing by eight o'clock. We'd play until two in the morning and I'd get home about three. On Saturday mornings I had to get up early to work on that farm all day. If I was lucky, we'd play again on Saturday night. I'd get in late again, then get up early on Sunday morning for the feeding and then church at eight o'clock.

After Sunday dinner was my time to snooze. There ain't nothing better than a Sunday afternoon nap. When I didn't get one it was hard to get through the week.

Things at school were running pretty smooth and the colored weren't being no trouble. The talk around Clayton was always about the colored. First they'd ask you if you had to sit beside one and then ask if the colored gave you any trouble, then they'd ask if the colored caused problems on their own. A lot of people offered to help take care of any colored that was giving problems. Everybody expected a full scale riot to erupt any day at school but it didn't happen. The main concern was the white girls and everybody always wanted to know if the colored boys was keeping their hands and eyes to theirselves. They were. The main problem seemed to be some white girls who were too friendly with the colored to suit some folk's taste. Mostly everybody at school just got along.

The first football game was a big deal cause it was the first time a team had been integrated. It was also the first time the colored didn't sit in their own section. In the past the white and colored high schools might play each other, but the stands were strictly marked off.

There were about ten police cars there for that first football game in September. Police in helmets and billy clubs walked around but nothing happened except a football game. The Homecoming game in October really scared a lot of people cause there were some colored girls nominated for Homecoming Queen and everybody was scared one of 'em would win instead of a white girl but that didn't happen.

Patty Sherman won Homecoming Queen, like everybody expected. Kathleen Holt was in the court. People were also scared to death a colored boy would escort a white girl but that didn't happen either. I didn't get to see the Homecoming game cause every Saturday in October I had to work cause October was the time for picking corn and combining soy beans and lespedeza.

I did see one football game in November. I went with Charlene. I wanted to go with Kathleen Holt and called her up the day before. When I called her house she answered the phone.

"Kathleen?" I said, surprised she'd answered.

"Yes, this is she," she said.

"This is Compton Gregory."

"Hi, Compton," she said. "How are you doing?"

"Fine," I said. "Would you like to go to the game tomorrow?"

"I'm sorry, Compton, I've already got plans to go to the game with some others," she said. "But thanks for asking."

I was stunned she said that but I said "You're welcome" then I said, "Good-bye" and she said "Bye" and I hung up.

It was a pretty big risk to call Kathleen and ask her to the game. I didn't know if at the last minute I'd have to do something on the farm or not. I worked extra hard that morning to get everything done I needed to do and then went to the game, which was at one o'clock then, right after the game, I went back home to do the feeding. We had to play that night, too.

I did see the first basketball game, which occurred on the Friday night just before Thanksgiving. Boy was that something. There were twenty-one policemen there—I counted them—and twenty of them had on helmets and flak jackets. The only one who didn't was the sheriff himself who walked around with just his uniform and gun. Everybody said the football games were alright cause they was outside and there was plenty of room to maneuver but inside at a basketball game with people piled on top of each other, well that was just asking for trouble so the local police came prepared to stop whatever it was that was brewing.

Actually, it seemed like the grown-ups were more likely to cause trouble than the kids so there wasn't nothing brewing except a basketball game. All the kids were just scared to death to even breathe with all that tension. There wasn't even much yelling and cheering except from the cheerleaders. Some local guys said they came out to help the police and they walked around mouthing off but the colored boys just turned and walked away from them. That must've been hard to do cause the white boys said some pretty nasty things. I reckon the colored knew they was outnumbered.

I always thought it wasn't very smart for those white boys to be so insulting to the colored. Suppose their car broke down in Tar Town, which is what we called the area in Clayton where most of the colored lived. Then what? If those white boys'd been outnumbered in a situation like that they might've gotten thumped, except the police were always pretty good about protecting whites from mean coloreds. Still, you never know when you're gonna need help or where it's gonna come from.

I have always found it hard to hate somebody I actually knew, unless they gave me a good reason for it. I never had any problem hating the colored before I went to school with them. I knew I was supposed to do that so I did. It's easy to hate people you never see but after we got integrated the colored in school never gave me a good reason to hate them, although I was always careful not to be too friendly and get called a nigger lover. I sat behind a colored boy, Michael Sheffield, in homeroom and I got to like him. Sometimes I almost forgot he was colored.

What amazed me most about the colored was that they weren't all alike. They could be so different when you looked at them as people. I had always thought of the colored as more or less one person. Couldn't even tell one from the other except for the ones that worked for us cutting tobacco but there are a lot of differences between colored people. That's not what I had been told when I was growing up. For instance, I never thought a colored person would like to read or be good at math or even like marching band or classical music. I knew they could play ball but was shocked to discover in gym class that there were some colored boys that weren't so hot at sports and didn't care about it neither. I thought they could all sing and dance too until music class.

I tried not to make it any harder on the colored than it already was. I figured they had problems enough without me adding to them. Besides, I had to work on that farm anyway. Aunt Tootie and Aunt Noodles and most of my relatives actually told me to keep clear of 'em and I did mostly. I did lend Michael Sheffield a pencil once when he lost his. Lent him fifty cents once for lunch cause he'd forgotten his money and I happened to have fifty cents on me, even though I brought my lunch to school every day in a brown bag.

Michael paid me back the very next day, which is not what I'd heard about colored. I was told you could kiss any money you gave them good-bye cause none of them wanted to work, which was why so many of 'em were poor, and that whatever money they did get their hands on they'd waste on cheap wine or something loud, flashy and useless. That's what Uncle Roadkill always said.

The biggest surprise of that whole last year in school was that the colored were just people. I'd never thought of 'em that way before but I saw some of 'em was scared sometimes and they worried about things. Had to get their homework done just like the white folks. They had feelings, too and those colored kids had mamas and daddys just like us white kids and those mamas and daddys cared about their kids like our mamas and daddys cared about us. Worried and fretted over 'em. The fact that the colored were just like ordinary people once you got to know 'em was a giant revelation to me.

Some of the other whites didn't feel the same way I did. They still called the colored kids niggers. I could never call a colored kid a nigger to his face cause I could tell it hurt 'em deep down. It wasn't my nature to go hurtin' people like that. Maybe it's because I didn't like being hurt myself.

Joe Stoneman and some other white boys in the senior class used to like to go out on Friday and Saturday nights and fight. They'd start with some beer and then try to find somebody to get into a fight with before the night was over. They tried that on some coloreds during football and basketball games but the coloreds stuck together and one time a group of colored boys even left a game early. Mostly Joe Stoneman and those other white boys like that ended up fighting amongst themselves.

Thirty-One

Some of the farmers were getting jobs to help make ends meet. By Thanksgiving Uncle Roadkill was working at the feed store and Jake Pursell was working in town at the Post Office. Daddy hadn't gotten a job yet but I knew he'd talked to some people cause I'd heard some whispers. I wasn't supposed to know any of that stuff so I pretended I didn't and then two weekends before Thanksgiving he come home and told us he'd gotten a job down at the Hardware Store. He'd have to work all day in the store and then do his farm work after he got home. He'd get Mondays off but would have to work Saturdays half a day. That meant he'd need me to work each and every weekend if we was to get all the farm work done.

Daddy started work on that Tuesday a week and a half before Thanksgiving and worked that whole week. The next week he worked through Wednesday and then got Thanksgiving day off. He said the work wasn't all that bad but it was hard being indoors all that time. It was also hard being chained to somebody else's schedule after he'd been his own boss for so long but sometimes you gotta do what you gotta do. This looked like it was something that had to be done.

On Thanksgiving Day it felt like old times. When we woke up the house smelled like food cooking. The weather outside was about as pretty as it could get. It was cool but there wasn't a cloud in the sky, which was as blue as a rich man's swimming pool.

Thanksgiving always started with the men hunting. Usually it was me and Daddy and Uncle Roadkill and maybe Uncle T-Bone and Uncle Soup. We'd get up early and head out at daybreak, hunting for quail, although I'd always shoot a rabbit if it jumped up in front of me, but it was mostly quail. We even left some corn and soy beans standing in the corners of the fields by the woods for the quail to feed on.

Hunting quail is mostly a matter of walking all over fields while the bird dogs—we always had pointers—circle in front of you until they smelled some quail. If the dogs found the quail they would stand or "point," just like a statue. We'd walk forward real slow in a line with our shotguns ready—we had 12 gauge with small bird shot—until the quail were flushed out.

Quail take off quick. You can't see 'em or hear 'em then all of a sudden they fly up with a whrrrrr sound from their wings. They fly straight and fast in all directions. You've got to get that gun on your shoulder, aim and fire and hope you're not shooting at the same bird somebody else is shooting. If they get to the side or behind you then you can't shoot cause you might hit somebody. Hunting quail is tough on the nerves but it makes you a good quick shot or else you don't get anything.

About a year ago on a school day along about the edge of dark Daddy and Uncle T-Bone came back from hunting with nothing. Hadn't even seen a quail to get a shot. I grabbed my shotgun and my dog, Rocky, jumped out the back of Uncle T-Bone's pick-up truck. We went through this little gully and patch of woods right beside our house and into a field. We hadn't gone 50 yards when Rocky stood; I walked up slow, flushed the quail and got one. All in about five minutes time. Daddy and Uncle T-Bone had hunted all day and hadn't even seen a quail, much less bagged one. Made me feel pretty good for being left out. That'll teach 'em, I thought.

Actually, the shooting is fun but the best part of hunting is just being outside, watching the dogs work and trying to outsmart those quail and being with people you like and just talking about stuff with grown men. That's what's great about hunting, being treated like a man.

My dog's name is Rocky and I remember when Daddy brought him home. He was just a little pup, mostly white with a brown tip on his tail, two brown ears and three spots on his forehead. I named him Rocky after my favorite baseball player, Rocky Colavito. The pup's daddy was Uncle T-Bone's dog, whose official registered name was Buck's Big

Boy but his real name, that is, the name everybody called him if they wanted him to come, was Mongo. Uncle T-Bone raised pure bred registered bird dogs and we'd gotten one from him before, a little female named Sugar. Uncle T-Bone rented out Mongo for breeding and sometimes got a pup back. That's how I got a full-fledged genuine registered pointer bird dog. Hise official name was Buck's Baby Boy but, like I said, his real name was Rocky.

I took to that dog soon as I got it and trained it as a 4-H project. It would sit and heel and lay down for me. That was a smart dog and when hunting season came the grown-ups took him out and he showed himself to be a natural. Almost as good as Mongo, who won Field Trial trophies and all that. Uncle T-Bone even took Rocky to some Field Trials but he never won first place.

When Rocky was about two years old some men came to our house and wanted to see him. Daddy knew 'em and knew they was coming and told me they was coming to look over Rocky. Said they'd heard how good he was and they needed a good hunting dog and wanted to enter some Field Trials.

When they got there Daddy turned Rocky loose in the field in front of our house. We kept Rocky chained up in the back yard cause you can't have farm animals and bird dogs mixed together. Well, Rocky went to work on that field, sweeping back and forth like a good bird dog should do, then they went over to the next field and the same thing. Daddy went along with the men but I just stayed in our yard watching. Finally, they come back in our yard and Rocky ran up to me. He jumped up on me and I petted him and all that. The two men hung around their pickup truck while Daddy came over to me.

"Son," he said. "They want to buy Rocky. They've offered $200." Then Daddy said, "It's up to you, son. He's your dog and it'll be your money."

Two hundred whole dollars was an awful lot of money. I'd heard some people had that much money but I'd never actually seen it. When Daddy told me that all I could think about was what I'd buy for $200. A new baseball glove—a really good one. A new bike. A new shotgun. I mean, heaps of things I wanted. I looked down at Rocky and all I could think about was getting stuff. But I didn't answer right away. I was holding Rocky and petting him and I looked up at those two men and they were standing by their pick-up truck just sorta shuffling around. One man had a leash rolled up real loose and he was holding it. They was watching me close.

I just kept going over what $200 would buy when Daddy said, "Son, you need to hurry up and make up your mind. We can't keep these men waiting all day." I wanted to say "Take him" but the words just stuck in my throat. Then Rocky stuck his nose under my arm and nuzzled me and I wanted to push him away and just get that $200 and be done with it so I stood up and looked at Daddy, opened my mouth and the words that came out were "I just can't do it." He just said, "I understand son. I'll go tell 'em." Then I knelt back down and hugged Rocky so hard. He just wanted to get away and run but I wouldn't let him. I heard one of those men say "That boy sure loves that dog" then the other one said "Hope he hunts 'em," then they got in the truck and was gone. Daddy just walked right past me and didn't say nothing, just went in the house while I stayed outside a little longer with Rocky.

That sure was a lesson in selling I never forgot. Anytime after that when I heard people talk about going into sales cause that's where the money is, well, I knew it wouldn't work for me. If I really liked something I wouldn't want to get rid of it and if I didn't like something I wouldn't want anybody else to buy it either so I was stuck, destined to be forever banned from the free wheeling easy money life of the salesman.

On this Thanksgiving Rocky found three different coveys of quail and we got them up. Uncle T-Bone was always the best shot and he got five. Daddy and Uncle Roadkill each got three and I got one. It was always a standing joke about me getting one quail every time we hunted and I did it again, but I did kill a rabbit too, and nobody else got one of them.

We got back to the house a little after noon and had to pluck and clean those quail. I skinned the rabbit and cleaned him and then we washed 'em all good and put them in the freezer and then about 1:30 in the afternoon we all sat down to Thanksgiving dinner.

Boy that was food fittin' to eat. There is always at least two kinds of meat—turkey and ham—for Thanksgiving. We also had fried oysters and some quail too. Trouble with eating quail is that you have to chew careful because there might still be bird shot in 'em. If you bit down hard on bird shot you can do serious damage to your teeth but it is a good, sweet meat. Sometimes we had a little deer meat on a platter too, mostly cause whoever had shot a deer was proud of it and wanted to talk about how they got it. It was a badge of honor to get a deer every year. Uncle T-Bone was the only one I ever knew who did it year after year.

Well, after all that food—like mashed potatoes and gravy, green beans, sweet potato casserole, corn, cranberries, biscuits and I don't know what-all—there was nothing to do but lay down and sleep. The bad thing about having company over for Thanksgiving is that you have to stay awake after the meal and talk to them but with family you just lay down wherever you flop and go to sleep. Daddy had a recliner and he'd lay back and snore so loud it would crack the ceiling. Uncle Roadkill laid down on the floor and he was almost as bad. Mama and the women folk always had to clean up the dishes first so the boys and men folk got a head start on sleeping. There ain't no better sleep than the sleep that comes after you've filled up your belly with a Thanksgiving meal.

Thirty-Two

On Thanksgiving evening Bunky Wathen called and asked if I could play on Saturday night. He was getting up a band to play at a bar called the Buck'n' Doe. The Golden Melody Boys had the regular Friday night gig at Gilmore's, but we didn't have a dance on Saturday night booked. So I told him I could.

I had been getting noticed for my playing. Bunky and some others had called before a time or two and asked me to play with them but I'd always had something set with the band when they asked. But this time I didn't.

I didn't really know Bunky all that well, although I'd known him all my life. He'd never spoken to me until I got in the Golden Melody Boys and then he got all friendly whenever he came to where we was playing. That was fine with me. I like to make friends with whoever's around, plus Bunky liked to talk about guitars and playing and I liked that too.

The rest of Bunky's band was actually a bunch of musical misfits. Scarecrow Robbins was going to play drums, Alton Wentworth was going to sing and play rhythm guitar, Bunky was going to play bass, and I was going to play electric take-off guitar. Scarecrow worked for the William P. Bretton Plumbing Company and liked to play the drums. The fact that he wasn't too good didn't bother him in the least. He freely admitted he had more nerve than talent but felt that most big stars were in the same category. Maybe that's why Scarecrow also insisted on singing some songs during the evening as well.

Bunky wasn't bad on guitar and was pretty good on bass. He could do a walking bass for a shuffle song as well as the standard thumb thumb bass most country songs required. Bunky wanted me to sing a few songs but Alton would be the main singer, which was a smart move on his part. Alton Wentworth is the best country singer I ever heard in my life, better than anybody I ever heard making records, but Alton Wentworth just can't stay sober or get his life together enough to be a singer.

We met at the Buck'n'Doe at six o'clock on Saturday evening, ran through a few songs, and were ready to play at eight o'clock. I'd get $10 for playing that night, which I thought was pretty good for just getting called up out of the clear blue.

The youngest member of that band besides me was 33 years old; I had just turned 17. It was an older crowd at the Buck'n'Doe but they all came to have a good time. Mama was scared for me when I told her where I was gonna play cause of all the shootings that had happened down there but I told her people don't shoot the band. I'd never heard of somebody in a band getting shot. Even in the wildest fights. Besides, the Buck'n'Doe had chicken wire around the stage for additional protection.

The band members that Bunky pulled together weren't quite as good as Billy Boy, Garner and Ardmore so I couldn't just jump up and do some song and expect them to follow, but Alton was a great singer so I just decided to lay back and follow whatever he did.

We started a little after eight o'clock and on the first song, which was an instrumental of "Down Yonder," Scarecrow's drum stick flew out of his hand, right out the open window beside him. It landed in the water outside. See, the Buck'n'Doe was built out over the water on Cummings Bay on some poles. Lucky it was low tide and the water was only about six inches deep where the drum stick landed.

Soon as Scarecrow's drum stick flew out the window, he stopped playing and jumped up and went over to the window. That made us all stop playing. "I lost my stick," he said. Then he leaned out the window and dropped his other stick. Course Scarecrow was pretty looped by the time we started so this adventure should'a been no surprise.

Well, that drum stick flying out the window put us all in a bind and we didn't know exactly what to do. Scarecrow only had one set of sticks so it was decided that since I was the youngest and the skinniest the other band members would hold me out the window by my ankles so I could pick those drum sticks up out of the water. I wasn't too excited about this idea but I'm glad to say it worked out all right. I crawled out the window, Bunky and Scarecrow took hold of my ankles and lowered me down, and then I fished around in that cold, dark, wet water until I found those two drumsticks. Soon as I hauled 'em in, and got hauled in myself, somebody shut that window. Scarecrow fussed cause he said he'd get too hot so we opened the window just a little bit.

We played mostly old songs that night. In fact, we played some songs I'd never heard of before that night but I could always find a take-off run to play in the song's break, even though it was a challenge. Alton could sound like one of them big old floor radios when he sang. Lawd, that man could evermore sing! I came in on some harmonies with Alton on the chorus, but our voices didn't blend like me and Billy Boy's. After awhile, I just let Alton carry the whole song cause my harmony vocals weren't really adding anything, at least not like they do when Billy Boy's singing. Besides, I just loved standing on that bandstand and hearing Alton Wentworth sing. He is that good, but Alton could only stay away from the alcoholic stuff as long as he wasn't in a barroom. He mostly stayed sober cause he stayed home. Alton was never able to take a social drink. That night he succumbed in the worst way.

Alton had a partial plate in his mouth—one tooth in the front. He was singing something when all of a sudden that partial plate with that one tooth on it shot out of his mouth in a long arc and landed right in the middle of the crowd of dancers. Well, the whole band stopped right then and there and Alton got cussin' something fierce about losing his tooth. Somebody picked it up off the dance floor and brought it to the bandstand and Alton took it and put it in his shirt pocket. He said he didn't want it flying out any more so he'd put it away.

Well, Scarecrow thought it might be best if somebody else held that tooth cause Alton might lose it so Scarecrow took that tooth and put it in his shirt pocket. Then Alton's wife came to the bandstand cause she was worried about that tooth so Scarecrow gave it to her and she dropped it in her purse. We started playing again and Alton hadn't sung three lines when he stopped the band. "I can't sing for whistlin'," he said. That spot where the tooth belonged was a hole now and Alton would whistle every time he tried to sing so I jumped off the bandstand, went over to Alton's wife while Alton was standing there cussin' about his tooth, and brought his tooth back and gave it to Scarecrow, who then gave it to Alton, who put it back in his mouth. After that, everything went pretty good, except Alton kept getting drunker and drunker.

At the end of the night Alton couldn't stand up. Scarecrow had to play the drums with one hand and use his other hand to hold up Alton from the back. If Scarecrow hadn't had his hand in Alton's back, Alton would've fallen right back into the drum set. He was a mean drunk too, so he wanted to fight everybody. After we finished playing we had to get him in his car to get him home. Now that was certainly an adventure. He'd swing at anybody and everybody who came close to him so we had to open the car door and try to let him back into the car while he was swinging at us. Finally, he fell in the backseat and I was elected to drive him home cause everybody else was too drunk. Well, I got Alton home with Scarecrow and Bunky following. Soon as we pulled in the driveway Alton turned into a perfect gentleman and got out of the car and walked straight as an arrow right into his house.

We was all standing in the living room with Alton's wife saying our good-byes and Alton was in the bathroom when all of a sudden we heard bottles breaking. We ran into the bathroom and there was Alton drinking after shave lotion and then throwing the bottles up against the bathroom wall. He must've had about five or six bottles of after shave and he drank them all. By that time his wife said it was best we should leave, she'd take care of him. She said she knew he'd beat her but she could handle it all right and it would be worse if some other men were around cause then he'd accuse her of cheatin' on him. That would make him worse.

So we went off out of there and I got home that night about 4 a.m. It was tough getting up at 6 to milk cows and do the feeding and it was hard to stay awake in church but Mama said if I was going to play those filthy honky tonks that I had to at least go to church on Sunday. That was not my first choice for a Sunday morning activity after playing music late on Saturday night but I figured it was the least I could do to keep playing music so I done it. Mama and Daddy were pretty mad about me playing the Buck'n' Doe so I did my best to please 'em that Sunday.

Thirty-Three

I had the chance to learn a lot about playing music that Fall. I started out just thrilled to death to be playing at all and full of myself for being up on a bandstand in front of people and gettin' money for not working but then I started studying what I was doing and figuring out how to sing a song or put on a show and work a crowd.

One night on TV I saw some guitar player put the guitar up behind his head and play so I decided to try that, too. Billy Boy sang "Jambalya" and the take-off guitar part wasn't too hard so I started putting my guitar up behind my head and playing the break. That went over like firecrackers. I'd do that two or three times a night. The only time it didn't work too good was late one night when I was in the middle of that part pickin' and realized I'd forgotten to put the guitar behind my back so I just grabbed my guitar and brought it up fast. Unfortunately, I was still looking down at the strings so I smashed myself in my own face with my own guitar. Felt pretty stupid doing that and Billy Boy and them laughed about it all the way home that night.

I learned how to sing a song on a bandstand. I learned how to change my phrasing on the ballads and pull out some notes longer and cut some others short. Roger Miller used to sing like he was talking and I'd do that some. Listening to George Jones taught me how to really pull on a note with my voice. I listened to a lot of George Jones records, studying his singing. I also learned how much I love to sing harmony, especially with Billy Boy. I learned how two voices can blend together so tight that it feels like they was woven together.

I learned that you can't be shy or backwards or scared when you get up on that stage. That's the way you might feel but nobody better see it. When you take that stage, buddy you better take that stage. You own it and you own that audience. You gotta be full of yourself and what you're doing, even if you don't know what you're doing. People in an audience don't like indecision.

When I took a stage, I learned to take all of it. You gotta get over being afraid of looking like a fool and just go ahead and play the fool. You gotta take chances in front of a lot of people and that gets awful scary but that's the way to entertain folks—just go out and grab 'em and hold on and don't let go. I learned all that from playing in front of audiences. I also learned you'd better do your practicing somewheres else before you get in front of people. People don't want to hear you practice, they want to hear you play. You can only get away with foolishness and messing around so long. People don't want to waste their time or their money on somebody who ain't no better than they are. People want to see talent.

I also learned that show business is work. The first night we played for six hours it was fun and we would'a done it for free. Coulda gone six hours longer. But after that it wasn't quite as thrilling. You have to pace yourself and plan on how to do a set. People want to party and dance and have a good time. At the beginning of the night we'd do two fast songs and then a slow one. Later, we'd do a fast one, then a slow one, then a fast one, then a slow one. If people were really liking a song, we'd just play the second half over again until it felt like it was time to quit. People don't like being forced to quit having a good time when they're in the middle of it.

We'd always end the night with three straight slow songs. You finish with a fast number and people's energy gets up and they want to keep on going so you have to cool a crowd down, let 'em down easy and leave 'em tired and exhausted. We wouldn't ever do a fast song at the end of the night. Even that last half hour wouldn't have any really fast songs—just medium tempo before the three ballads.

I learned that when you sing a song you've got to believe what those words say. At first I just sang the words and was glad I knew 'em, then I got to realizin' what those words were saying and that people felt those emotions that were sung so I started learning how to act out a song, to be the person in that song instead of somebody on a stage that just knew the words. If I sang a song, I felt it. If I didn't feel it I wouldn't sing it, unless we had to do it as a request, but I made sure I had feelings to put into every song I sung. Without those feelings that song wasn't much more than just a sound.

What I really learned was how much I love singing and playing in front of a crowd. I guess the only word to describe it is hunger. I just had a hunger to get out of those tobacco fields and get up on some stage and perform. Wanted to see some action at night rather than stay on that farm and look at stars and listen to the silence of the wind blowin'. It was a hunger I had that said there's more to life than just cows and dirt and tobacco. There's music playin' somewhere and people laughin' and dancin' and I wanted to be part of all that. Wanted to be having a good time instead of feeling so lonesome. Lonesome and too tired to do anything about it. That's what farming is all about, but playing music—especially playing in a band—is energy and excitement. Bright lights and big cities. Playing music and singing with somebody like Billy Boy when your souls and spirits just seem to blend together when you get that right song and the music is carrying you along like a big ocean wave and your voices blend so tight together that it feels like you've been touched by angels. Playing and singing country music in some place where there's people to listen and dance and feel that music touch them. That's where I want to be.

Farms are dark and lonesome and quiet. Oh, Lord, let me hear music playing in my life. That's what I want and that Fall I got my first taste of it.

Thirty-Four

A week before Christmas we had a big snow and Mr. Bloodworth and a young woman (Daddy said it was his girlfriend) ran off the farm road in the middle of the night. We didn't know about it until next morning when we found them in their car. The car had run out of gas so there was no heat and Mr. Bloodworth's toes had been frost bit. The doctors at the hospital thought they were going to have to take the toes off but then they didn't.

Taking off Mr. Bloodworth's toes was a big deal that everybody talked about. I kept wondering why it was such a big deal cause you don't really use your toes that much. It's fun to let mud soak all around 'em and I guess it would slow you down running but Mr. Bloodworth didn't run anyway. Daddy always said the town folk oughta know what we knew about Mr. Bloodworth cause then they wouldn't think he was so high and mighty.

When Mr. Bloodworth got drunk he always ended up at his mansion pretty much laid up passed out. Whenever he'd come to he'd call Frog or Tadpole Wendell to bring him more liquor and they'd do it for awhile and then one day you'd see an ambulance come and haul him off. Daddy said they took him to Richmond and dried him out. He'd be gone a couple of weeks and when he came back he'd be straight up sober and real nice. You wouldn't a-thought anything had happened. Mr. Bloodworth himself never let on anything had happened. He just went on his business like it was business as usual.

That was a big snow and we had to hook up a snow plow Daddy built for the tractor to get off the farm. Daddy was up early working on that cause he had to get to work at the hardware store. Good thing he had that snow plow because he said the store was overrun by people wanting snow shovels, rock salt and stuff. Daddy never had much respect for people who didn't plan ahead. That night after he finished working at the store he come home for dinner and fussed about all the people who never thought about snow till it was laying on the ground. He sure wasn't like that. He'd built that snow plow in the summer.

We all got presents that Christmas. I got a pair of pants and two shirts for school, which I never liked to count as presents cause they weren't toys or fun but I sure needed 'em. Just before school started we'd always get some new clothes and this year I got two pair of pants and three shirts and I'd worn them every day. My shoes from last year were still good but getting a bit tight but there weren't no holes in the bottom so they was alright.

I also got a record album of Johnny Cash, one of those hand games with b-b's in it, a model car to put together, two pair of sox, an orange and an apple. We always got an orange and an apple at Christmas. Daddy always said that the biggest thrill during the Depression when he grew up was getting an orange and apple in the dead of winter. I think that was mostly all they got. That's why he passed on that tradition to us.

Christmas Day was usually spent visiting relatives after the presents was opened. The kids always got up real early and one year I remember I got up at four o'clock but since I wasn't a kid no more now I slept in till 6:30. Daddy said I'd earned it. Then I went over to the barn with him to do the feeding and milking before we went back to the house and opened the presents.

Mama cooked us up a big breakfast and then we just sat around until noon when we went up to Granny Gregory's for a big feed with Daddy's side of the family. When we got there Uncle Roadkill had already drunk about a third of the egg nog Granny had bought for Christmas. That egg nog was so full of whiskey that it stung your throat when it went down. Uncle Roadkill kept saying it ruined good whiskey when you poured it into egg nog but it seemed like it just changed the coloring a little.

Granny always had the best hard candy at Christmas. It was like cylinders with a painting on the end, like a rose and Lord I love peanut brittle and she always had plenty of that, too. Uncle Roadkill used to say that every Christmas Granny fixed a meal that could've fed the Russian Army. This Christmas wasn't no different and everything she fixed was thoroughly fittin' to eat.

I still didn't get to sit with the grown-ups, who filled up the big table pretty good. I ate with the cousins in the next room and we tried to listen to what the grown-ups was talking about. It was mostly talk about who got what for Christmas but every now and then Uncle Roadkill would start talking about how bad it was that us white kids had to go to the same school with niggers. That upset him pretty bad. I wondered if the colored families were having Christmas dinners with their relatives and saying the same things about their kids having to go to school with whites but I'd learned not to think too much about all that stuff. I was living in the middle of all that and I'd learned to roll with the flow. Going to school with colored didn't bother me one bit. It was people like Uncle Roadkill who were outside looking in that seemed to have the most trouble adjusting to it.

It looked like it was going to be a typical family gathering. After dinner the men kept drinking egg nog and getting meaner while the women washed the dishes. Every now and then it would get kinda quiet and then I'd hear Uncle Roadkill take off on something else, like the Viet Nam war or hippies or something and everybody would sorta nod in agreement even though they weren't as loud or troublesome about it as he was. After the women finished the dishes Mama came into where us kids was all sitting around and said we had to go over to her side of the family for awhile.

Daddy was kinda woozy drunk by then. The drunker he got the more he insisted he wasn't drunk at all but even if he was stone cold sober he'd never let a woman drive if he was in the car. Somehow he got us over to Grandma Hevington's house. It was about six o'clock when we got there. That place was a whole 'nother adventure altogether.

Aunt Tootie, who had been pretty quiet at Granny Gregory's, and Aunt Noodles was blowing a full gale when we walked in the door. Their husbands, Uncle T-Bone and Uncle Nick, were just sittin' in the corner in a warm glow with pretty stupid grins on their face. They were talking about Nadine Brookline Thompson, who'd had her baby on December 7. Mr. Brookline, who'd served in World War II, insisted on naming the baby and he named it Pearl Harbor Thompson. Aunt Tootie said the baby looked more like a group portrait rather than any one person in particular. Aunt Noodles said that wasn't because Frankie Thompson was two-faced either. Both said it would probably take a series of blood tests to find out who the baby's real father was.

Nadine had gone up to Wendall's Bar, which is in the back of the store, by herself on Christmas Eve. She'd told Frankie she needed to pick up a few things at the store. Aunt Tootie said that no truer words were ever spoken. There was seventeen guys from the Army in that bar and after Nadine walked in she turned around and locked the door and nobody come out for four hours. Tadpole Wendell, who was tending bar, stayed there and watched everything. When it was all over he said that the Army should give Frankie Thompson a medal cause he'd laid down his wife for his country.

On Christmas morning Frankie and Nadine got in a fist fight in her folks' living room and fell into the Christmas tree. They knocked it down and busted it all up. Meanwhile their baby kept crying and wouldn't shut up. Mrs. Brookline, who took care of the baby, was fixing dinner and asked Nadine to do something about the crying. Nadine went into the bedroom and shut the door. All that fuss had caused Mr. Brookline to start drinking heavy. Just before dinner he came into the living room and just fell down passed out right on top of the Christmas tree, which was laying in the middle of the floor. Mrs. Brookline unplugged the lights and served dinner. They just let Mr. Brookline lay there on the living room floor and snore while they had Christmas dinner. Aunt Tootie said Mr. Brookline snored a twelve on the Richter scale.

It amazed me how much Aunt Tootie and Aunt Noodles knew about other people's Christmas before the day was even over. They knew that Junebug Glaser had given his wife a shotgun for Christmas. He told her he was going to borrow it whenever he wanted to go hunting. At dinner he got tanked up and then went outside and was shooting his wife's new shotgun to test it out. He hit the TV antenna so now nobody there could watch TV and Junebug was in no condition to get up on the roof to fix it neither.

Leola Lippitt has bought her new husband a brand new pick up truck for Christmas. He bought her a box of chocolates. Leola ate that whole box of chocolates right after she opened it looking for a diamond hidden in one of them. It wasn't nothing but a box of chocolates and that made Leola mad so she ran out in the yard crying and started pounding that pick-up truck with her fists. Uncle T-Bone said "I hope

Leola didn't scratch up that brand new pick up truck with those long finger nails of hers. Nothing worse than a brand new truck with scratches."

Mama said, "Why in the world would somebody put a diamond in chocolates? Suppose there had been one and she'd a swallowed it?" Aunt Noodles said, "Why would Leola buy somebody a brand new pick-up when she can't afford to put gas in that beat up wreck she's driving?" Aunt Tootie said it was because Leola Lippitt's corn bread wasn't quite done in the middle.

Thirty-Five

I had to play Christmas night with the band at Dollar Bill's in Lynnville so I had leave the Hevington's get-together before things had gotten going good so I could be in Lynnville by seven o'clock to help set up the bandstand and run through some songs. The party at Dollar Bill's started at nine and Mr. Billington—his real name was Bill Billington—was expecting a big crowd.

The thing I've always hated about Christmas is Christmas songs. I never was too good at playing 'em or singing 'em and I didn't really enjoy trying. I'm not a Scrooge or anything, I like Christmas songs just as much as the next guy as long as somebody else is doing them. They just seem like the kind of songs that should be done by a high school chorus. And they are but the music teacher never let me in the chorus so I guess that left a bad taste in my mouth about Christmas songs, but even if I had'a been in the chorus I still wouldn't have enjoyed doing Christmas songs on a bandstand.

At that Christmas dance we had to do "Silent Night" and "Jingle Bell Rock" and "Blue Christmas" and we even did "What Child Is This" as an instrumental. Funny thing is that people danced to all the Christmas songs. There was people wanting us to play "Joy to the World" or "Come All Ye Faithful" or "O Holy Night" but we wouldn't even try those. Can you imagine a country music band doing those things? I think some folks just wanted a sing along. Lucky for us, most people wanted to dance.

That night while we was playing there was an older lady, she must've been at least forty or more, who was feeling her oats. She wasn't drunk, but she sure didn't have any inhibitions. She kept coming up to the bandstand and asking me to dance with her. Well, I kept saying "No, I can't. I'm playing in the band" but she kept coming back. Then one time she came up from behind me and I didn't see her. She grabbed the neck of my guitar and just took it off me. I still don't know how she did that so quick but she took that guitar off and there I was standing there looking like a fool. Then she says "I reckon you'll dance with me now." There wasn't nothing for me to say except "I reckon so" and I danced with her a little bit but then I got back to the bandstand in a hurry. The rest of the boys in the band was laughing something fierce when I got my guitar back.

On the way home Billy Boy and I was riding with Shock. Garner was riding with his girlfriend and Ardmore was with his newest true love. Shock said, "Did you enjoy your dance with Mrs. Pennington?"

"Who's that?" I said.

"That's the lady you danced with. The one who took your guitar off you."

"Oh, her," I said. "I didn't have much choice, did I?"

"I thought you was going to get lined up with a Pennington girl. That would've cost you your guitar!"

"What's a Pennington girl?" I asked.

Shock laughed but he was the only one who did. Me and Billy Boy just looked at each other.

Then Shock said, "Oh, Lord. I don't know what to tell you two. Don't know how much you know already."

"Well, so far not much," said Billy Boy.

"That's obvious," said Shock. "I'm just not sure I should be the one to tell you."

"You mean tell us what a Pennington girl is?"

"Yeah, well, sorta," said Shock. "You see, that woman you danced with, Mrs. Pennington, has a roster of girls she manages and some of the biggest wheels around are her customers. Her girls are always very young, very pretty, and very expensive. Now do you know what a Pennington girl is?"

"Yea, I get it now," I said. "I had no idea who she was. She just seemed like she was having a good time."

"Yea, she was," said Shock. "I'm not sure why she was there.

Maybe Christmas night is an off night for her and she took the chance to get out and enjoy herself. I don't reckon many of her clients call her on Christmas. They're mostly rich and respectable, so they have to stay home on Christmas."

"Were any Pennington girls there tonight?" asked Billy Boy.

"I don't think so," said Shock. "I think Mrs. Pennington was there by herself. If there'd been any Pennington girls she'd a been doing business instead of just having fun."

And that's how me and Billy Boy first heard about Mrs. Pennington and Pennington girls.

Thirty-Six

On New Year's Eve we got to play the big dance at the American Legion Hall. This was Big Time for us. The American Legion charged about $10 per couple and we got top dollar that night—$250 for the evening or $50 each.

We'd never seen money for one night like that before and we all figured if we could make that kind of money every week, we'd all be full-time professional musicians. Course, we figured only the top country music stars could make that kind of money on a regular basis but it gave us something to dream about.

We started playing at 8 o'clock and people were havin' a grand ole time. We got to take a 10-minute break at 9, 10 and 11 cause they wanted to sell lots of drinks so it kinda made it hard to really get going. Our band liked to get into a set and really play hard for about two hours before we took a break. That way the dancers were just exhausted and so was we but it all felt so good.

We were supposed to play from 11 straight through until 12:30 and of course we had to play "Auld Lang Syne." We did it as a sing along and then as an instrumental with me plunking out the melody on the bass strings of the guitar. After we took the break at 12:30 the folks lined up for a big feed. It was mostly breakfast stuff but we had to play "softer" music—that's what they told us—while people was eating so we played some instrumentals and mostly ballads.

We cranked it up again when people finished eating until ten minutes to 2 in the morning when there was last call for alkee-hall and everybody had to load up on drinks for the rest of the night. It was against the law to sell booze after 2 a.m. but not illegal to drink it so that's when they sold whole bottles of whiskey and stuff. Then we played until 4 a.m.

Well, here's where the real adventure come in. Sometime around ten o'clock that evening Arlene Longworth came in that dance just swishing herself like you ain't never seen. She is married to Delbert Longworth and has three little kids at home. She had gotten married real young—I think she was pregnant in high school so she got married when she was in the eleventh grade. Then her and Delbert had three kids bam bam bam right in a row. When she sashayed in the door that night she was 22 years old and a real looker. Her husband, who everybody called Poor Old Delbert, is eleven and a half years older than her. Aunt Tootie said he was a little bit slow on the draw, too. In fact, Aunt Tootie said that Delbert Longworth was so slow on the draw that if he'd been in a cowboy movie he'd been shot dead before the picture started. Aunt Tootie oughta know what she's talking about cause the Longworth's lived right beside Leola Lippitt, and those two houses was right across the road from Uncle T-Bone and Aunt Tootie.

Arlene come down to the dance by herself and didn't mind asking any man there to dance with her and Lawd, she danced up a storm. She'd swirl around on that dance floor and that dress would go up and you could see her legs all the way up to the top of her panty hose. She didn't pay no never mind to who was looking, either. Course, it got pretty awkward because that dance was mainly couples and a lot of the women there didn't care much for Arlene dancing with their husbands or boyfriends. You could just see those women trying to rein their men folk in from Arlene but Arlene never paid attention to the women there. A lot of the men were on a toot and just having a ball so Arlene took advantage of that. They probably caught hell when they got home, though.

It was just after two in the morning and we'd finished our break and I was up on the bandstand there playing take-off guitar on "Just Because," a song Billy Boy sang but I had a lot of hot pickin' to do. I was pickin' fast and furious, looking down at my strings when Arlene jumped up on that stage and flung both arms around my neck and then she stuck her tongue in my ear. She also squished herself tight against my guitar and deadened my strings so I couldn't play a thing. My arm was smushed right between my guitar and her breasts. They was nice and soft.

After she'd licked my ear right there on the bandstand—I couldn't do nothin' but stand there and enjoy it—she said "Let's go get a motel room." I just said "O.K." before I even thought about it and she looked at me with a big smile. By that time Shock had come up and was pulling her off the bandstand.

When she got off the bandstand, I went back to playing but mostly I was in shock. First, I had to finish playing and that wouldn't happen until 4 a.m. Next, I had said "O.K." accidentally without really thinking about it and, finally, she was married.

I was still playing "Just Because" when she jumped back on the bandstand, grabbed my arm and said, "Come on. Let's go!"

"I can't," I said. "I'm playing."

"I want to play some, too," she said. She had just started to put her arms around my neck when Shock pulled her off the bandstand again.

Boy was my mind in a turmoil. Here it was a little after two and we couldn't quit until four and then we had to pack up and Arlene Longworth wanted to go to a motel with me right there and then. The worst thing is that part of me wanted to put down that guitar, jump off the bandstand and chase her just as fast as I could while another part of me said "Whoa, now, you're gettin' yourself into a mess that's gonna explode big time."

I wished I hadn't said "O.K" so fast cause I really didn't mean it but Arlene thought I did and that complicated things quite a bit. Arlene would come up to the stage, point her finger at me and give me *That Look* and everybody in the whole place caught on pretty quick to what *That Look* meant. I just stood there with my guitar grinning like a chessy cat while inside my brain I was trying to figure out what to do. Billy Boy and Ardmore and Garner kept lookin' at me and grinning but I could tell Ardmore was jealous cause she wasn't falling over him, even though he'd brought a girl along that night to admire him while he played the drums. Still, Ardmore had his pride.

The more I watched Arlene dance the more I realized what a bad idea it was to go to a motel with her. First, there was the problem of the motel. There wasn't one for about twenty miles around and I'd never checked into a motel before so I didn't exactly know how to do it. I'd always heard you needed reservations so I wondered if maybe I should call when we quit at four and make some reservations. Then I tried to figure out what I'd tell the motel person when they answered the phone. I'd seen a sign out front of that motel that said "We rent by the hour" so I was trying to figure out how long it would take us to pack up, then how long it would take to drive there so I'd know what time we could get there and then what time we'd have to leave.

Then there was the problem of Aunt Tootie and Aunt Noodles. I was sure they'd find out if I left for a motel with Arlene Longworth and next day their tongues would be waggin' faster than a hound dog's tail at feeding time. But my major concern was that I'd given my word to Arlene and I felt obligated to keep it. Daddy always said that if you couldn't trust a man's word then you couldn't trust that man. That's exactly what he'd say, "If you can't trust a man's word, then you can't trust that man." I wanted to be trustworthy.

I didn't want to hurt Arlene's feelings, either. It was obvious she was counting on me real strong to leave that dance with her and I hate to let anybody down so I had pretty much decided to leave that dance with her, go to the motel room for an hour and talk to her. I thought she could probably use some coffee so I was trying to figure out how to get her some when we got to the motel. At the end of the hour I'd take her back home and everybody would be happy and everything would be all right. She wouldn't feel embarrassed or disappointed like she would if I just ignored her. I'd tell Aunt Tootie and Aunt Noodles that I was just doing Arlene a favor if they started gossiping about me and her. I had decided it would be sinful to be involved with a married woman so I would resist Arlene's advances and explain I didn't want to take advantage of her just because she'd had a few drinks. I'm sure she would thank me later. When it was over her husband would be happy I'd brought her home safe and sound and I would feel like I'd kept my word and done the right thing by not hurting her feelings or embarrassing her.

For about the next hour and a half Arlene kept dancing and I kept playing. I also kept going over in my mind what I was going to do when I quit. I'd help the boys pack up the equipment and then I'd open the car door for Arlene, then I'd put my guitar in the trunk and we'd drive off.

There was a big old clock on the back wall of the American Legion Hall and I looked straight at it from the bandstand. Arlene was standing right in front of the bandstand giving me *That Look* while I was singing the Jim Reeves ballad, "Four Walls." I looked over the crowd dancing at that clock and it was eight minutes to four. That's how come I saw

Delbert Longworth as soon as he come in that building.

Delbert and some of his buddies had been duck hunting about a hundred miles away that day so he was dressed up in his duck hunting outfit with hip boots, camouflage hat, and a big hunting coat with the head of a dead duck hanging out of each of his side pockets. I could tell he was mad by the way he looked and the way he walked. I found out later that he'd come home that evening and Arlene wasn't there. Her sister was baby sitting the kids and when Delbert asked her where Arlene was she sent him on a wild goose chase or two. Finally, he ended up at the American Legion Hall's New Year's Eve party after several hours of driving around the county and checking out other places.

Delbert Longworth walked through that crowd of dancers like they was a bunch of bushes in a swamp. He swung his arms to clear a path and took big, long strides in his rubber hip boots all the way till he got up to Arlene, who never saw him come in. He grabbed Arlene by the arm, spun her around and, without breaking stride, hauled her out of there. She started crying and whimpering about him squeezing her arm too tight but Delbert never said a word, just walked out the door and let it slam shut while the whole floor of dancers, who had stopped to watch the whole spectacle, just stood there. Then everybody turned and looked at me. I made sure that I sung every single word of "Four Walls" like it was the last song I'd ever sing on earth.

At four o'clock in the morning, after we played "Old Lang Syne" one more time, we quit and put the equipment in Shock O'Connell's truck. It was twenty-two minutes after four when we finished packing up and I was standing on the front steps of the American Legion Hall with my guitar case in my hand. I was tired but relieved. I had thought Delbert Longworth would'a thanked me for getting his wife home safe but when I saw him walk in that door I knew he'd a shot me before I'd had a chance to explain what I was doing with his wife.

It was a sobering, scary thought to be dead at seventeen years old. I vowed to be more careful next time a married woman stuck her tongue in my ear while I was playing on the bandstand.

I didn't want to go to bed, even though I'd been up all night, but I knew I needed to head home so I took a deep breath and drank in that winter air and gripped my guitar a little tighter. That was how the year 1966 began for me.

Thirty-Seven

The Golden Melody Boys started playing at The Captain's Corner on Friday nights right after New Year's. The club was just outside Boscoe and was owned and run by Mrs. Pennington. Shock said he landed that job for us because Mrs. Pennington called him looking for a country music band and he convinced her we was the one to hire.

The first Friday night we went there we was walking up to the front door with our arms full of equipment when Paul Benson came out on the front step. Paul is Mrs. Pennington's bouncer, a great big man, about six foot six and must weigh about 250 pounds. Mostly muscle with a huge beer gut. He come out the front door holding some little skinny guy by the shirt collar and the seat of his pants, carrying him like he was a bag of trash. When he got to the front step, Mr. Benson just tossed that little guy into the the air and he landed on oyster shells, just like some bag of trash had been tossed outside, and then Mr. Benson said, "If you're going to drink you can stay but if you're going to sleep then get the hell out." Without missing a beat Mr. Benson saw us and said "Come on in boys. We're rarin' to rip to tonight."

Like a lot of other places we played, The Captain's Corner was located down by a bay—this time it was Blue Bottom Bay—and the whole parking lot was covered with oyster shells. Outside the bar was a big sign that said "The Captain's Corner. Mrs. M. A. Pennington, Proprietor." We walked up a long set of steps and inside was a juke box, pool table and a long bar. The Captain's Corner served booze and seafood. All summer long they'd serve hard crabs—hot, steamed Blue Crabs that people would pick and eat. In the winter there'd be oysters and they'd have Oyster Scalds. That's when you drop this wire bucket filled with oysters into boiling water for about ten minutes before you serve 'em. They come out like raw oysters, only hot, and the hot water gets the shell to open up just a little bit so's you can get your oyster knife in there a little easier. Talk about fittin' to eat! There was never no better living than an Oyster Scald on a cold winter night.

The band was starting to feel like pro's at this music business now so we went in, plugged in the amps, Ardmore set up his drums, and at 8 o'clock I kicked off "Walk on By" with my guitar. Beer and drinks was always on the house for us—we never had to buy a drink as long as we played there. Billy Boy liked to drink and so did Garner, but Ardmore only had a beer or two a night. I hardly ever touched the stuff. The only reason I did take a drink now and then was cause it was always sitting there and sometimes I couldn't get a soft drink and I was thirsty. People never would buy you soft drinks, they always bought you beer but sometimes Miss Pennington came through and made sure I had a ginger ale. She always said, "If you're going to drink a soft drink, at least drink one with a little class. Don't drink a Big Orange or Root Beer—that was what I'd ordered at first—always drink ginger ale."

At the Captain's Corner we made $40 apiece each night—that included each band member as well as Shock, who always got a full share of what the band made. He earned it, too. If it wasn't for him, we wouldn't'a played nowhere. This was good money and we thought we'd died and gone to Heaven.

The first night at the Captain's Corner was a cold, clear night in January. We drew a pretty good crowd—almost a hundred—and they started dancing almost as soon as we started playing. Sometimes it takes a crowd an hour or so to warm up and start dancing. But not this bunch—they were ready to hot foot it from the git go.

About 11 o'clock that night a woman with four little kids come in and she was in a rage, stompin', carrying a huge black pocketbook. She went right through the dance floor where everybody was dancing and over to a table in the back where some men were playing cards. See, at these bars there's always at least one table set up in the back where men play poker. They play all night long on the weekends.

The little kids looked like they'd been drug out of bed, all sleepy and wearin' pajamas and rubbin' their eyes. This woman went over to the card table and walked up to one of those men and yelled out "You sonovabitch." Then she started beatin' the hell out of him with her purse. He jumped up from that table and headed towards the door and she followed right behind him yellin' and cussin' and hittin' him with that purse. Those little kids were just like a parade, following their mama and daddy. She was yellin' "You said you would be home after work" and "You better not have lost your whole pay check" and "Your damn dinner is still sittin' there cold waitin' for you" and stuff like that.

We played The Captain's Corner for six straight Friday nights and that same woman came in with those same kids and got that same man the same way every single Friday night. I never could figure out why she always waited until about 11 o'clock to do it. But it was a regular event and it got so we began to look forward to it after awhile.

The first night we played at The Captain's Corner I thought it was just a regular bar but about half way through that night I learned it was actually two places. The bar we played in was a regular honky tonk, nothing out of the ordinary but behind that bar was another, secret bar. You got to that one through an underground tunnel. I didn't know about the tunnel until Mrs. Pennington showed it to me and Billy Boy one afternoon—she said she couldn't show it to us at night.

The other place was a real classy place, with thick carpets, expensive chairs and big chandeliers. That's where her "girls" stayed. The whole place was underground and the only way to get to it was either through a secret tunnel from The Captain's Corner or through a parking lot about a hundred yards from the bar. This parking lot was surrounded by a big wall and the gate had a special call box. People would drive up to the call box, say a password and the gate would open, then they'd park inside the wall and go to what looked like a little room in the middle of the parking lot. There they'd have to say their code word into another box for that door to open, then they'd go down a stairs to get into Mrs. Pennington's Parlor, as she called it.

The Parlor was a fairly big room with hallways running off from it and rooms on the hallways. Mrs. Pennington's customers would meet the girls in the Parlor and then go back to the room with one or sometimes the customer knew which girl he wanted so he'd just go to the room and wait.

On the last night we played at The Captain's Corner, me and Billy Boy took Garner back to the secret parking lot and climbed up a bank so we could peek over. You won't believe this but as soon as I got to where I could see over the wall who did I see getting out of his car but Mr. Bloodworth.

Billy Boy and Garner each said they saw the Mayor of Lynnville when they looked over, but I didn't.

Thirty-Eight

On a rainy Saturday afternoon in early March me and Daddy was sitting in the barn stripping tobacco when we looked out the window and saw a car drive up to the house. It was Aunt Tootie and soon Charlene come running across the field to us. My cousin, J. T. had been killed by an automobile. He was twelve years old.

J. T. and his twin brother Randy was Uncle Soup and Aunt Fussie's boys. They was walking along the state road on the shoulder when Mr. Honeycutt came along and struck J. R. from behind and threw him a good ways. He missed Randy.

Mr. Honeycutt was drunk that day. In fact, he generally stayed that way. It wasn't really his fault, he couldn't help it, and everybody knew that. When he was sober everybody liked him but then he'd just sneak off to himself and get drunk and nobody could stop him. He couldn't even stop himself. That's what happened that Saturday.

Mr. Honeycutt had almost killed another cousin of mine, Shelton, who was Aunt Noodles and Uncle Nick's boy. That had happened a year ago in February. My Uncle Nick worked at a service station and drove their tow truck. One night he got called out to clean up an accident on McEntire Bridge. Shelton was fourteen at the time and went along with his Dad. They had hooked the wrecked car up to the tow truck and was ready to haul it away but first they decided to pick up the broken glass and other stuff laying in the road. It was about eleven o'clock at night.

That's when Mr. Honeycutt come out of the night driving fast. When he got to the bridge he never even slowed down. He said later he never saw them. Mr. Honeycutt's car hit Shelton and throwed him up against the bridge wall. That broke Sheldon's pelvis and laid him up a long time. Now this very same Mr. Honeycutt killed J. T. Gregory.

Soon as Charlene told us, me and Daddy went to the house and washed up, then we all got into the car and drove over to Uncle Soup's and Aunt Fussie's house. Uncle Soup was just sitting in the living room with his head buried in his hands and he wouldn't look up. Aunt Fussie was crying loud and hard with her head on Mary Dean Maggard's shoulder.

We learned that J. T. was dead when he got to the hospital but Randy said he saw J. T. breathing when they put him in the ambulance. His mama, that's Aunt Fussie, said it was good that he suffered for his sins but also good that he didn't suffer too much. You could tell it sure tore Randy up real bad. Him and J. T. was real close, stayed together constantly, was never apart. It was like they was one person, really.

We wasn't at Aunt Fussie's house long before Mama and them was on the phone talking to people and letting everybody know what happened. By night time the neighbors was bringing over food and stuff. That night Daddy and Uncle Bubba stayed with Uncle Soup while Aunt Fussie's sisters came and stayed with her.

The funeral was on Tuesday so all us cousins was at school and couldn't go. That just seemed to make matters worse for the family. The cousins were all supposed to go to school that day and sit there and just not think about that funeral with one of their own kin dead and being buried. You might as well told a rooster not to think about crowing.

The grown-ups just buried J. T. by themselves. The grown-ups said that something like this wasn't the kind of thing you was supposed to talk about so just leave it be, but J. T.'s death and funeral was all the kids at school could talk about. I don't think the grown-ups in my family could even talk about it amongst themselves.

At the funeral home Uncle Soup had a picture taken of J. T. in his coffin. After the funeral he got it made into an eight by ten, framed it and put it on top of the television set in the living room. For months after that Randy would have nightmares every single night and wake up screaming.

I didn't see J. T. buried and I didn't see Linda Connor buried either. Those were two people about my age who died that year and it made me know what it feels like to be old and have people you know die. It don't feel too good. Like Old Man Death is real close to you which, of course, he is all the time but you just don't know it or think about it.

Linda Connor died about two weeks after school started in September. She had got spinal meningitis somehow before school started and then went down from there. We never did see her at school that year—she had it before classes started. The health department came to school and had everybody tested and Lord, wouldn't you know it but Imogene Fielder, who always put on a big show anyway, got to grabbing her chest and touching her head and complaining about all the symptoms they told us to watch out for to see if any of the rest of us had it. Imogene got hauled out of school for a couple of days and had a bunch of tests run on her in the hospital but everybody knew all along she was clean as a whistle. Healthy as a horse but with all the sense and personality of the horse's rear end.

I didn't go to Linda's funeral cause Aunt Tootie made a big deal to everybody about getting a dead person's disease. Actually, it hadn't actually ever really been decided I would go to the funeral, but I wanted to and I knew some of the kids at school were going but Aunt Tootie got to talking about how you can get a dead person's disease just by going to their funeral cause their germs float all around their coffin and in the air. Aunt Tootie said the dead person's relatives probably had a good dose too so it wasn't safe. You were bound to catch something, especially if you was a kid. Grown-ups didn't have to worry so much about those things because they was old enough to be immune to most children's diseases. She convinced Mama and Daddy that it was better for all the kids to just stay home, which we did.

Thirty-Nine

The rain in March helped get the tobacco in order for us to strip and then pad it. Tobacco hangs in the barn until it's dried out and then when it rains the dried brown leaves of the tobacco become soft. We call that "coming in order." When tobacco gets "in order" you take it down out of the barn and pull the plants off the wooden sticks and tie up the stalks in bundles of twenty-five sticks. If you try to do that when it's dry the leaves just crumple up into powder.

Those bundles of tobacco are put into a storage room between the tobacco barn and what is called the stripping room. Then you cover the tobacco with canvas and sprinkle water over the canvas to keep the tobacco soft and in order.

Stripping tobacco means taking the leaves off the stalk, then tying the leaves together in bundles, but you have to sort out the leaves while you're doing this. Like, me and Daddy will sit in the stripping room, which is a small room, about eight feet by ten feet, with a wood stove to keep us warm. That's important cause you strip tobacco in the winter.

We always have a radio plugged into the wall. That's the only pleasure you get stripping tobacco, listening to that radio. The first time I ever heard a Beatles song was in the stripping room one Saturday in early January, 1964. There was a big hullabaloo about the Beatles coming to America and Tex Taylor, the disc jockey on the Saturday afternoon country music show was talking about them. He was mostly fussing about their hair and them being foreigners then, right in the middle of his country music show, he played "I Want To Hold Your Hand." A little while later he played "I Saw Her Standing There."

You won't believe this but during that same afternoon he played both of those songs again. His show went from dinner time at noon until sundown and that's what we always listened to while stripping tobacco. Every time he'd play one of those songs by the Beatles he'd come back on the air and you could almost see him shaking his head and then he'd say, "Whew, I don't know what anybody sees in that."

He just didn't understand it but it lit a fire in me. I love country music but I love the Beatles too and I made up my mind they was good despite what my relatives said right after they'd been on the Ed Sullivan Show. I still can't believe the first time I ever heard them was on Tex Taylor's Saturday Afternoon Country Music Jamboree.

The first person stripping tobacco takes off the best leaves towards the bottom of the stalk. Those are called "firsts" and you always have your best man doing this cause this is the most important job. Those leaves are the oldest and biggest and sell for the highest amount. The next man gets the "seconds" which are the second best leaves on the stalk, then somebody strips the "tips," which is the little leaves at the top end of the stalk. Those are the youngest and smallest and sell for the least amount when you take tobacco to market in the spring. Then there's always the "scraps," which are the torn up leaves, usually down at the very bottom of the stalk. The guy who strips the "firsts" always takes off the "scraps" too and just drops them down at his feet until he's got enough to make a bundle.

Stripping tobacco isn't all that hard but it sure is boring. You just sit there, usually on a keg turned upside down with a gunny sack over it or some kind of stool and do that all day long. That's how I spent my Saturdays in the winter when tobacco came in order.

After the tobacco was stripped, the bare stalks were taken outside and put in the manure spreader. When the manure spreader was full, you'd hook it up to the tractor and spread those stalks all over some field where they'd rot.

The bundles were a handful of tobacco leaves with one leaf wrapped around the top to keep them all together. That tying leaf would be wrapped around the top of the leaf stems a number of times to make it real tight then the end of the tying leaf would be tucked between the leaves in the bundle to hold it. It was a real trick to tie a good bundle so it looked good and would hold.

The bundles are always stacked behind you when you're stripping tobacco until there was a big pile and then they was taken out into the barn. There, you'd put those bundles on tobacco sticks and hang them up again in the barn. They'd hang in the barn until another rainy, wet day when they got soft from the moisture and then you'd take them down and "pad" them.

When you "pad" tobacco you get those big baskets, about four feet square with the sides curved up just a little bit, and lay them down flat on the ground, then you sit in the middle of the basket and start layering those bundles down in a special way. First, you start in one corner and keep putting the bundles down flat and let them overlap as you go around the basket in a circle, then you fill in the middle of the basket now and then to make it solid. By the time you finish the basket of padded tobacco is about four feet tall and the bundles are all packed tight so they won't come out. After you finish a basket, you jump off and get a gunny sack that's been cut open with a string tied to each of the four corners. You throw that burlap sack over the top of the basket of tobacco and then tie down each corner real tight to hold it all together solid.

The baskets of tobacco are kept in the barn until it's time to sell them. That's when the trucks from the tobacco warehouse come down and load 'em up and take them up to the warehouses in Boscoe. There, the buyers from the tobacco companies walk along the aisles behind an auctioneer and bid on them. That's how you sell your tobacco.

The part I always hated most about raising tobacco was them cold wet days in the barns. Sometimes in January or February every whole weekend would be spent in a cold barn. It was especially bad when you were taking the tobacco down off the stick. Somebody would get up in the barn and hand the stick with the plants of dried tobacco down to somebody on the ground, who would stack them in piles of twenty-five each.

The next step would be for one person to pick up the stick of plants, push the tobacco plants to one end of the stick by raising your knee against the tobacco on one side of the stick and pushing with your hand on the other side. That way you'd run those plants together in a bunch at the end of the stick. Then you hold up that stick towards the guy helping you, and he'd pull those plants off the stick and put them in a pile. When you had twenty five sticks of tobacco in a pile, you'd tie them up together with twine to take to the storage room to wait for stripping.

It would be so cold in the winter in those barns that your hands would be frozen stiff even with gloves on and you couldn't feel a thing.

You'd get splinters in your hands from those tobacco sticks but wouldn't even know it until your hands thawed, then you'd look down at your hands and see yourself bleeding or big long pieces of wood sticking in your hand but until you warmed up and thawed out you couldn't feel a thing. Once you got warmed up with splinters in your hands, woo-wee would that hurt like crazy!

Forty

On the first Saturday night in April the Golden Melody Boys played at the Boscoe Fire Hall for the Men's Softball League banquet. It was a fund raiser where some people got awards. We was supposed to start playing at 8 o'clock.

The band met over at the O'Connell's house but Shock couldn't go that night. He had to go out of town that day to pick up some electrical supplies for his business and wouldn't be back until Sunday afternoon so we packed our gear into Ardmore Pinworth's parent's station wagon and headed to the Fire Hall, which was about 30 miles away. We thought of this as a "road" gig cause it was so far away.

Billy Boy and I was sitting in the back seat of the station wagon and soon as we took off Billy Boy pulled out a jar of clear liquid that looked just like water. "It's moonshine," he said. Then he took a sip and passed it to me.

I hardly ever touched a drop of liquor but since this looked just like water I went right ahead and took a great big gulp. Wouldn't you know that stuff raced down my craw and right into my stomach where it burned so bad and was so powerful that it didn't stop at the bottom of my stomach. Instead, the stuff went right through my stomach, down both my legs and all the way to the very tips of my toes. When it got to the end of my toes it bounced all the way back through my body straight up to the top of my head. At the top of my head it turned into a rubber ball and commenced to bounce back and forth inside my body from the toes to the top of my head and back again.

There was tears in my eyes when I gave that jar back to Billy Boy and he took another sip, then handed it back to me. One sip should've been enough to teach me a lesson but I was determined to correct my first mistake so I took another sip, this one a little lighter. This time it felt like I'd swallowed a warming brick and there was a warm glow inside me.

The moonshine filled up about two-thirds of a Mason jar. Billy Boy and I sipped on that stuff all the way up to the Boscoe Fire Hall. I didn't feel a thing the whole way except it burned my throat a bit whenever I swallowed but when we got to that Fire Hall and stepped out of the station wagon my legs couldn't hold a single pound of me and I collapsed right on the ground. Same thing happened to Billy Boy.

Well, that put the band in a major mess cause we had to set up but neither Billy Boy nor I could even get up off the ground. Ardmore and Garner had to set up the whole stage that night and boy was they mad. When they had everything set up, me and Billy Boy couldn't get up to walk in and play. By this time we were woozy as fuzzballs and couldn't even think straight, much less walk a straight line.

Lucky for us the banquet went into overtime. That let Ardmore and Garner get us some coffee and pour it down us until we got to the point where we could get up and walk and even play but we didn't want to. We just wanted to go to sleep but we had to play music until two in the morning.

We started playing and people started bringing us mixed drinks. Billy Boy said the best thing we could do to cure our hangover was to drink some of those mixed drinks. He said it counteracted the booze already in us and that we had gotten to the point where drinking made us sober instead of drunk. I believed him and started sipping on the mixed drinks.

Garner was mad that me and Billy Boy had gone and done what we done so he started drinking everything people put on the front of the stage then, right in the middle of one of our songs, Garner just got up from his steel guitar and walked off the stage. Went to the bathroom, I think. Of course, we just had to keep playing. At the break, we went looking for him and found him in the bathroom leaning up against the wall. He had a greenish color in his face.

That was a pretty rough night. Billy Boy said that more booze would cure my sickness so I took my medicine in healthy doses. So did Billy Boy. We mixed it up pretty good; some beer, some whiskey, some rum. You name it. Whatever people brought us, we smiled and said

"Thanks" and took a swallow. By the end of the night we was what you call falling down drunk. We did the best we could to pack up and carry out the equipment. Lucky some of the folks dancing stayed and helped us and we was lucky that Ardmore stayed stone cold sober the whole time, but boy was he mad.

When we got back to the O'Connell's house we got the station wagon unloaded. Actually, it was mostly Ardmore that done that, then me and Billy Boy and Garner got in the front yard and we all threw up. I thought I'd hit a gusher. It was pitiful, disgusting and a great relief. When I finally quit I got in my car and drove home wearing a cold sweat. I vowed the next time I ran into some moonshine I'd drink it cautious.

Forty-One

There's nothing like the smell of fresh turned black dirt in the spring and feeling those warm southern breezes after months of having that winter wind come from the north and cut through you like a cold steel razor blade. To look around and see trees come alive with buds, then one day see those trees filled with leaves a-growing. See the color green coming back to the land after a winter of grays and browns. There ain't nothing more beautiful on this earth than the earth coming back to life in spring.

I love the smell of stuff growin', the wet green smell of new plants and I love the sounds of spring gettin' busy with birds singin' and leaves blowin' in a heavy breeze and crickets chirpin'. The feeling that the whole earth is busy growin' into a new year. Spring is a beginning, a new start, the season of promises.

In spring you want to be outside on a tractor, in a field where you can breath deep and take the new air deep inside you. It's a time when you want to work hard all day long, doing stuff with your hands and getting dirty then, in the evening, you set outside and feel a coolness coming back as darkness settles around you. You can't set out in the winter and watch a day end, but you can in spring and summer.

In spring you feel the days getting longer, stretching a little bit more every day like a piece of leather that you're pulling on hard.

There's nothing like a spring Saturday when you get up early and get out in a field on a tractor with a plow and spend your whole day turning over the earth. Watch those birds fighting each other for the worms you've just served up to them on a silver platter. Or a day you spend planting corn or soy beans. Getting to the end of a row and carrying those hundred pound bags of fertilizer to fill up the corn planter or spreader. Smelling that sharp acid smell of that gray fertilizer. Carrying a five gallon bucket filled with corn or soy beans for the planters. A day of hard work like that and you sleep good at night. It's a solid, restful sleep where your body collects rest and stores it up for the next day.

In the spring I worked hard after school every day cause every minute counted. Daddy didn't get home until four-thirty and we had to do a full day's work in a couple of hours. We'd work hard Saturday and sometimes on Sunday, too. With Daddy working at the hardware store, we had to give up going to church on Sunday mornings cause our time for planting was so short and precious. Daddy said he thought the Lord would understand.

When kids are growing up the grown-ups always like to ask them what they're gonna be when they grow up. Mostly kids say they want to be what their Daddy is or maybe something a little exotic like a fireman or policeman. When grown-ups started asking me that, I didn't have an answer. I knew I didn't want to be a tobacco farmer. That was just too hard with not enough fun, but I really didn't know what I wanted to be.

Then, when I was in the fourth grade, somebody asked me and I just said "movie star." Don't know why I said it, really, except I knew that it was useless to ask a kid what he wanted to be when he grew up. Still, you had to have an answer. The response from adults took me back. Daddy said it was foolish to even think about stuff like that but the more I thought about it, it didn't seem so far fetched. Not that I wanted to be a movie star but some kid growing up was going to be a movie star, so why not me? Also, I realized that if you're going to be something like a movie star then you have to start with the idea of doing it, the dream. That's the first step. Get yourself to believe it and then others will start to believe it and if you believe in something enough, it just might happen.

That's what I was feeling about country music that spring. I wanted to be a country singer and I was doing it. Sure, it was on a small scale but it was the first step in the dream. People that heard me play and sing didn't mind believing I could do it either. It was easy for them to believe I could do it and the more I played and sang the more I believed I could play and sing country music for a living.

I once thought I'd like to have a job where I didn't break a sweat, one of those office jobs I'd heard talk about. Uncle T-Bone works for the telephone company and sometimes I thought I might like to settle for that. He's inside people's houses a lot working on phones. Has to climb poles a lot, but it sure beats cutting tobacco out in a field on the hottest days in August. A life with no sweat. That's what I thought would be The Good Life.

Now I feel like The Good Life is a life of hard work, but doing a work you love and enjoy. I wouldn't mind working hard at country music. I'll admit that spending six hours on a bandstand on a Saturday night ain't the same kind of hard work that farming tobacco is, but if you're going to be good at country music, or anything for that matter, you've got to do some hard work for it. The catch is that if you love what you do, it don't seem like work at all. That's like one of those secrets to life; love what you do and you'll never have to work. I love playing and singing country music.

It would be a dream come true if I could spend my life in country music, to be able to make a living singing and playing. Still, I know that even if I could spend my life in country music, and make a great living doing it, I'd miss the farm in spring. I wouldn't miss farming the rest of the year, but I know I'd miss that wind and dirt and rain of the spring when the earth raises up out of its winter grave.

Forty-Two

The Golden Melody Boys broke up in the spring. We'd played almost full time since September when we started at Gilmore's. I'd made enough money to pay off Shock O'Connell for my guitar by the end of the year.

We played The Captain's Corner every Friday night for three and a half months, until the middle of April. And we'd played a dance somewhere every single Saturday night in January, February and March. But then in February Garner got his notice from the Army for his physical and he passed it. In March he got his draft notice and was supposed to report for basic training at the end of April. Billy Boy decided to enlist in the Navy after Garner got his notice and he had to report for basic training on the second Monday in May. Ardmore started going to doctors to try to get out of the Army as soon as Garner got his notice. Aunt Doodles said the only problem with Ardmore was that he had a bad back. "Had a yellow streak right down the middle of it," she said.

Ardmore finally found a foot doctor that said he couldn't march, I think. Anyway, Ardmore' physical was in May and he came back and said he was out of the service. The foot doctor's letter had done it. Course, Ardmore kept referring to his "foot problems" and "bad feet" all the time. Aunt Tootie said Ardmore wouldn't have minded going to Viet Nam if they'd covered the country with mirrors.

A lot of guys in my high school class started trying to sign up for the National Guard but it was pretty full by the end of Spring, 1966 and the Guard wasn't taking anybody new. Except if your father was a Big Wheel or you knew somebody important. That was a good way out of the Army and everybody that could take it took it but by spring, 1966, the Guard had a waiting list a mile long for ordinary folks.

The last time the Golden Melody Boys played together was at a dance at the American Legion Hall in the middle of April. By this time we'd added another member to the band. Bobby Boy Lindsley, Billy Boy's brother, was playing bass. He couldn't actually play but Billy Boy wanted him in the band. He said he was leaving for the Service and wanted to play in a band with his brother before he left. Lord knows we needed a bass and on the songs where there was just the regular country thumb thumb bass it sounded good.

Billy Boy said anybody could play the bass but what he meant was that anybody could find the note of the chord the rest of the band was playing. That's all Bobby Boy did when he played the bass but he couldn't play a walking bass for a shuffle or even do a step up for a chorus. Bobby Boy could find the note of the chord being played and that's the note he played, no matter what the song was.

The dance at the American Legion doubled as a going away party for Garner and Billy Boy. We had a grand ole time that night and I let Billy Boy sing lead on all of the songs. It had gotten to the point that sometimes him and me got into a argument about what song we'd sing or who would sing lead but that night I just sang harmony the whole night and it felt so good and so right to hear our voices blending. I knew I'd miss that sound. It was High Lonesome at its best and we both vowed that as soon as he got out of the Navy we'd get together again and form another band. That would be four long years.

On that last night I played a medley of the Army song, "The Caissons Go Rolling Along," the Navy song, "Anchors Aweigh," the Marine song and the Air Force Song and everybody loved it. It was real patriotic. Then we sang "God Bless America" and even did "Auld Lang Syne," even though it wasn't New Year's Eve. It was tough to see it all end and those guys leaving. It was especially tough on Shock O'Connell. He'd been talking about us all going to Nashville that summer and trying to break into the country music business and audition for the Grand Ole Opry. I must admit I was looking forward to that myself except I didn't know how Daddy could spare me on the farm. The Army and Navy solved that problem.

Daddy was real busy working at the hardware store and then coming home and farming, too. Uncle Roadkill said he stopped by the hardware store and saw that Daddy was busier than a one armed wallpaper hanger. I could tell it was taking a toll on him to be working at that store and farming. Sometimes he looked like he was about to give out.

I was going to school, working on the farm, and then playing music on the weekends, but after the middle of April when the band quit, it felt like I'd gone on vacation for a couple of weeks. Actually, with Spring planting it was a good thing I didn't have to play music for two weekends cause I don't know how I would've fitted it all in. Still, I missed the music, even though I played the guitar every night when I come in from farm work and I kept on writing songs.

Both Billy Boy and I was writing songs by then and sometimes we wrote songs together. We even worked some up with the band, but we never played one of our own songs on the bandstand in front of a paying crowd. Shock O'Connell said they was good but we should save them for Nashville. Billy Boy said he wanted to wait until Buck Owens did one and then we'd do it. He said he wasn't sure if they was really any good or not, that we might be fooling ourselves into thinking they were better than they really were. He said ole Buck Owens knows a good song and that's all he sings so if he done one, we'd know for sure it was good. Then we would do it ourselves.

The dance at the American Legion Hall was the last time we played together but Mrs. Pennington had a going away party for us. She held it up at The Captain's Corner on a Sunday afternoon. Part way through the party she told Billy Boy she had a special going away present for him and led him down to her Palace and gave him the pick of the pack. Billy Boy said it was the hardest choice he ever made. When he come back up to The Captain's Corner about an hour later he had a grin on him so big and broad he couldn't get it off his face, even if you'd'a hit him over the head with a baseball bat. Mrs. Pennington said she'd give me the same present before I left for basic training.

I wanted to get together another band after the Golden Melody Boys broke up but I just didn't know who else to call and I never was too good at organizing things. Shock O'Connell was good at that but, with Garner gone, he just wasn't much interested any more. Then, the second weekend in May I went and played a coffee house in Callwell, which was about 60 miles away. There was a college in that town and I woulda never gone and done that on my own except Shock told me about it when I asked him about getting together another band. He said they was a bunch of hippies and freaks and it might be a weird experience but it was worth a shot. I've always liked adventure so one Friday night I drove up there.

There was a bunch of guys with long hair in the place but they was pretty nice. It was a small place, just a big room really, with little bitty round tables scattered around and chairs against the wall. They sold coffee and apple cider and that was about it—no booze—but a funny smellin' smoke hung in the air. They was open Friday and Saturday nights and Sunday afternoons and I went up there three times that first weekend, then the next weekend and the next weekend and I played every time I went up there. All you had to do was ask the guy running the place and he'd write your name down and when it came your time he'd call your name and you'd get up there. Pretty loose.

That coffee house was a whole new lesson in singing and songwriting. First, you stand up there by yourself, with just a guitar, and you have to put yourself over without a band. People in a coffee house sit and listen—they don't dance—so everything I'd learned about playing for dances—how to work a crowd—just got filed away and I had to learn how to move a crowd with words instead of a rhythm and a beat and that was an important lesson.

That's when I started listening to Bob Dylan cause that's who that crowd talked about all the time. They talked a lot about politics, which I didn't know much about, but if you got them talkin' about music, it was always Bob Dylan. I learned some of his songs and did them, like "Don't Think Twice, It's All Right" and "Love Minus Zero/No Limit," which was a weird title for a song because those words weren't even in it. They always went over well. Some of those songs were so long but when you sing by yourself, you don't have a band to carry you and there's no instrumental breaks—so the words have to carry the songs. That makes you work harder when you write a song, cause you gotta keep piling on words and images and painting a picture with the lyrics.

That's when it struck me that the first line of a song was the most important cause you really had to hit hard with that. I've spent a lot of time working on the first lines of songs but here's the killer—the first line has to knock you out, then the second line's gotta be even better and the third one's got to top that one—so the listener keeps listening. If you just throw in a line to get to the end—and I'd done that, I must admit—you lose your audience.

The music has to drive too, has to keep the audience interested, so that's where I started looking for surprise chords, which is what I always called them, something unexpected, outside the three or four chord country structure. And the melody has to surprise you—not jolt a listener—but keep them interested. If you want to learn songwriting, then write some folk songs. Songs that tell a story and paint a picture for an audience when all you've got is just your voice and a guitar.

That folk song period connected me to an audience in a different way. The folk singers looked like the audience and you sang with them, not to them. I liked the idea of setting myself apart on that bandstand and being a star, escaping the audience cause in the Golden Melody Boys I was using the music to get away, but I learned you got to unite with your audience. If you're going to succeed, you have to sing what they're thinking and feeling and you have to learn them as people, not just a mass of faces. People expect a singer to be their spokesman. You're not just living your own life, you're living theirs too. They don't want to just listen to you, they want to agree with you and, in a way, they need you to tell 'em their own feelings, speak out what's troubling them or what makes 'em feel good. Those couple of weeks singing folk music taught me that and I learned it all by myself cause nobody else went to that coffee house with me. I can always get along with whoever is around and wherever they're at but some folks just can't get used to things and people that are different and those folks in that coffee house was way different than the people who listened to the Golden Melody Boys. They sure was an open-minded bunch; anything was all right with them.

The last time I saw Billy Boy was on the Sunday just before he left for the Navy's boot camp. His folks had a party outside at their house and grilled up some hamburgers. Billy Boy and me pulled out our guitars and sang some songs for about an hour that afternoon. I remember that the last song we sang was an old gospel song, "If We Never Meet Again This Side of Heaven." Billy Boy must've been feeling religious that day cause he wanted to do a lot of gospel songs and I sung harmony on every one.

Billy Boy Lindsley's leaving was the biggest event in my life. I felt like I was saying good-bye to part of me that Sunday and I could tell he wasn't all that crazy about going either. Course, we joked about me joining the Navy too so we could form a band and sing on ships.

On the farm, the only thing eventful that happened in all of May was the electric fence. We had electric fences around our pastures because they was easy to put up to keep the cows in. Daddy was always saying not to touch it cause it could electrocute you and I was always real careful to avoid it. One time I watched Buzzy Harwell pee on the electric fence and he danced and yelled pretty crazy.

Well, one day I was going under the fence and my shoulder touched it and I felt the current just rush to one side of my body. I just fell down on the ground and lay there cause I knew I was dead. I was on my back, looking up at the sky and the clouds and all, just waiting for Jesus to come and get me. I laid there and laid there and was thinking that dying wasn't so bad after all and that it wasn't much different than living but the sky never changed much and Jesus never came. Finally, I realized that I could feel the ground beneath me and the grass was starting to itch and then it occurred to me that I wasn't dead at all. I'd only had what's called a near-death experience.

Forty-Three

The Honor Society at the high school held its induction in May. The whole school was let off for the afternoon and everybody sat in the auditorium. The lights went out and then the Honor Society members took some lit candles out into the audience and gave them to the new members, who then came up on the stage. It was all a big surprise and you never knew who was going to be named.

I knew I was going to be in the Honor Society. I'd worked hard for it. It was hard to work on the farm and play music but I always did my school work too, even when it took me a couple of hours.

In the mornings I'd try to study or read on the bus but that was hard and I usually didn't succeed. That was one rowdy bus and if the other kids caught you reading or studying they'd call you a sissy or steal your book or generally make it so's you couldn't do nothing like that any more but every now and then, like when there was a test, I'd sneak a peak at the book to go over some stuff and sometines I had some notes on a piece of paper folded up in my pocket that I'd pull out.

I'd gotten all A's and B's in high school except in Chemistry, which was a real struggle. But I'd passed. I'd gotten almost all A's my senior year but the guy who taught Trigonometry, Mr. Wysler, was the faculty advisor for the Honor Society and he was mad at me. I'd taken typing instead of trigonometry because I figured I'd need typing and I didn't know any other way I'd learn it. I wasn't so sure about trigonometry, but Mr. Wysler said I was dodging the hard stuff and taking the easy way out.

I was a little nervous as I sat on the bleachers at the school assembly. I watched the Honor Society students take their candles and fan out in the audience and I wondered which one would be the one to come to me. I knew 'em all but I wasn't real good friends with any of them. They were mostly girls and I knew one girl came from a farm family too but her Daddy owned his land.

Two Honor Society students walked past me with their candles and then a third came down towards where I was sitting. There wasn't anybody behind her so I knew she must be the one to get me. When she got up to me I tried not to be surprised and kinda looked away. She was walking real slow, like she was looking for somebody so I straightened up a bit and then looked at her so she'd know where I was. She looked at me but then looked further down the line of students and then walked past me a little ways. She kept looking at the bleachers trying to find somebody and I kept looking at her to let her know where I was when she looked back. Finally, she made some quick steps and walked over to Robert Barnes and gave him the candle. Robert Barnes is colored.

I was stunned and I don't remember much about the rest of the ceremony. I wanted to cry but didn't want anybody to know I was disappointed so I didn't say nothing to nobody. When I got home that day I told Mama they'd had the Honor Society induction and I wondered why I didn't get it. "Could you ask them why?" I said.

She told me "You can't question people about that. They make up their minds and pick out the ones they want and that's the way it is. It's just up to them and you can't question 'em."

The Honor Society induction was on Wednesday and it took until Friday before I finally got up the nerve to go into Mr. Wysler's classroom after school to ask him why I didn't get in. The classroom was empty and he just looked at me when I walked in. I was shaking and scared and maybe he knew it.

"Well, Compton," he said. "What can I do for you?"

"Mr. Wysler," I said, and you could hear my voice breaking, "I was just wondering if maybe you could tell me why you thought I didn't make the Honor Society." That seemed like too many words to say but I couldn't stop them coming out. I wasn't sure they all made sense either, but I knew he knew what I wanted to ask.

He looked at me for a little while and then he said, "Compton, you just aren't involved in many school activities and we like to see well-rounded students who are involved in things like sports and clubs and the yearbook and those sorts of things." I just stood there and didn't say nothing.

"But my grades are pretty good," was all I could say.

Mr. Wysler waited a bit before answering. "Yes, Compton they are. Although you took the easy way out this year." I knew he was talking about the typing course.

"And grades aren't everything, Compton. There's character too and that's an important part of being in the Honor Society. We have to make decisions, not just on grades, but on things like school activities and character. We have to see that someone is succeeding in more than just their school work. We want to see activities outside the classroom, too."

So that was it. They just didn't want a character like me in the Honor Society. But all I said was, "O.K. I just wanted to ask."

And Mr. Wysler said, "Sure, Compton."

Forty-Four

There were two school buses that went by Wendell's store. There was my regular bus and then there was one that went up towards Boscoe driven by Mr. Hurly. Mr. Hurly wasn't supposed to stop at Wendell's but sometimes in an emergency he'd let me ride his bus and I'd get home about the same time as my regular bus, although Mr. Hurly left later. When I left Mr. Wysler's room I walked down the hall and into the lobby to wait for Mr. Hurly's bus. I sat down on the tile floor just around the corner from the Principal's office. I wasn't trying to hide or nothing but I guess that's what I did cause Mr. Wysler came down into Mr. Levitt's office and they started talking right inside Mr. Levitt's door and I could hear everything.

"Compton Gregory just came into my room and asked why he wasn't chosen for the Honor Society," said Mr. Wysler.

Mr. Levitt gave a little chuckle laugh and then said "Did you tell him the Honor Society does not solicit white trash?"

"Well, I didn't actually use that term," said Mr. Wysler and you could almost see a smile on his face when he said those words. "But I believe I conveyed that he wasn't Honor Society material."

"Good, good," said Mr. Levitt. "I'm proud of that Honor Society. Those are good families." And then he said something that was sort of a compliment. "Compton does seem like he's a decent kid, but he comes from white trash." There was a pause and I let that soak in and tried to figure out how to take it. Then Mr. Levitt started again. "White trash breeds white trash and he plays that white trash music, which leads me to believe that he won't change. Those kind never do. They won't make something of themselves and then they breed more of the same. Sometimes he seems like he's a cut above some of those other white trash kids. Then again, an apple never falls far from the tree."

I wasn't sure what apple trees had to do with it but the rest of the message was pretty clear. I liked my folks but he sure didn't. Besides, I didn't have any choice who my relatives were. That was beyond my choosing.

Then Mr. Levitt said, "I went to school with Mitch Hevington, Compton's uncle. He killed himself when he got out of the Army. I'll never forget the day I heard about that. It was right after Christmas."

"Is that the one who was queer?" asked Mr. Wysler.

"Yes," said Mr. Wysler. "Queer as a three dollar bill. None of us knew that while we were in school with him. Apparently it all came out in the Army, and then he was out with one of his drinking buddies and made a pass at his buddy."

That would've been Herbert Hoover, I thought.

"The buddy apparently said he was going to tell everybody what Mitch had tried to do. That's when Mitch killed himself."

"That family's had a lot of tragedy," said Mr. Wysler. "One of his young cousins was killed this spring. Run over by a car, I believe. That was awful."

"Not as awful as what happened to Elton Hevington's wife and son," said Mr. Levitt. "She took their son and put him up for adoption and a couple in California, I believe, got him. Nobody ever knew their names or where they lived—that was part of the deal. Then she moved away—disappeared—and nobody's heard from her since."

"Yes, well wife problems run in the other side of family too, I've heard," said Mr. Wysler. "Didn't two of those Gregory brothers marry the same woman?"

"Yes," said Mr. Levitt. "Mary Agnes Kincaid was her maiden name and she had married Oliver Gregory when she was quite young. Then they split after a short while—only a couple of months really—but never got a divorce. Then Orville—that's the one they call Roadkill—came home from Army boot camp and married her just before he was sent to Europe. He returned from the Army during Christmas, 1945. The war was over and they were sending boys home. Over the holidays he found out she'd been married to Oliver before she'd married him."

Oliver was Uncle Soup. And I'd heard Uncle Roadkill had a wife once but nobody ever told me about her. In fact, nobody ever told me any of this.

Then Mr. Levitt continued, "Around seven months after Orville got back from the Army, Mary Agnes had a baby. At first he thought it was his, that it had just been born a little early, and they named it William."

Another cousin? This was the first I heard of this.

"But then Orville discovered the baby wasn't his, didn't he?" asked Mr. Wysler.

"Yes," said Mr. Levitt. "That child was actually fathered by Othello, another of Orville's brothers."

Othello was my Daddy.

"Whatever happened to that kid?" asked Mr. Wysler.

"When Orville found out he wasn't the father, he and Mary Agnes split and went their separate ways. Neither one wanted the child, considering the circumstances and all, so they gave it to a family who took the child in."

"Wasn't that the Lindsley family?" said Mr. Wysler.

"Yes, the Lindsley's didn't think they could have any children so they adopted little Billy then, later, they had a son and daughter of their own."

"I remember Billy Lindsley," said Mr. Wysler. "He was in my science class a couple of years ago. Barely passed."

"He graduated a year ago," said Mr. Levitt. "I've always wondered how, but the teachers all swore he managed to pass everything right at the end. I still think a few looked the other way on some of his tests, though."

"Well, you can't blame me for that," chuckled Mr. Wysler. "He didn't take Physics his last year."

"No, I'm sure he didn't," said Mr. Levitt.

Then Mr. Wysler said, "Mary Agnes has certainly made a name for herself since that time."

"She certainly has," said Mr. Levitt. "You ever been up to her place?"

"No way," said Mr. Wysler. "I've heard her prices are way beyond a high school teacher's salary."

"Yes," said Mr. Levitt. "A Pennington girl is quite extravagant but it lets Mary Agnes Pennington make a good living."

"Now there's white trash if you ever want to see it," said Mr. Wysler.

"Yes, but she's white trash with a lot of money," said Mr. Levitt.

Mr. Levitt and Mr. Wysler both laughed after that.

There was a whole mix of feelings inside me for a little while, then I just started to feel numb. I probably couldn't have moved if I'd had to which, lucky for me, I didn't have to. Mr. Wysler and Mr. Levitt never saw me. After they finished talking Mr. Wysler left the office and went back down the hall. I could hear his footsteps and I guess Mr. Levitt just went back into his office.

After I got over the numbness it felt like there was a knife right through my heart. I never hurt so bad in all my life. The bus drove up in a little while and I pulled myself up and got on it and just sat there in a seat near the back. No matter which way I moved I felt that knife inside me.

My face was just plain ordinary. Nobody could see nothing on it and that's how I worked to keep it cause I didn't want nobody to know what was inside. Deep down my heart was crying as hard as it could cry and there was a buzz inside my mind. I knew if I talked I just might cry out loud so I didn't say nothing to nobody all the way home. Just sat and stared out the window.

Forty-Five

Mama said if I didn't go to the Senior Prom I'd live with regrets my whole life. She said it was a once in a lifetime event and I said I was glad it only happened once and with a little luck I'd miss it.

The Senior Prom was the first Saturday night in June and I kept hoping somebody would call me to play a dance that night, but it didn't happen. Then, about two weeks before the Prom I decided I'd go so I called up Kathleen Holt again. I hadn't called her up in a long time and I hardly spoke to her in school but I was still in love with her.

The phone rang twice and she answered it. "Hello," she said.

"Kathleen?"

"Yes, this is she," she said. I thought that was a real high class way to talk.

"This is Compton Gregory."

"Oh, hi, Compton," she said.

"I was wondering if you'd like to go to the Prom," I asked.

"I'm sorry, Compton. I've already got a date. Perhaps you could ask me for something else?"

"O.K.," I said. "Good-bye."

"Bye, Compton." And I hung up.

I didn't know what to make of her saying "ask me for something else" and I just couldn't think fast enough when she said it to come up with anything. I'd have to ponder on that later. Meanwhile, Charlene asked me if I had a date for the Senior Prom and I told her no. She said that Julie Minter didn't have nobody to take her and she really wanted to go. Julie's dad is a dentist so I figure she must be rich. Julie is in Charlene's class; I know who she is but not too good.

"Do you want me to fix you up?" asked Charlene.

"Yea, sure," I said.

The next day Charlene came and said "I've talked to Julie and she'd like to go with you, Compton. So go ask her."

"Why should I ask her?" I said. "I thought that you were going to do that. In fact, I thought you just did that."

"Well," said Charlene. "I did ask her and now you have to ask her."

"If you asked her, why should I ask her?"

"Compton, you just don't understand."

"No, I don't," I said. "Tell her I'll be by the night of the Prom at seven o'clock."

"No, I'm not going to tell her that," said Charlene. "You have to tell her that but first you have to ask her, Compton. Girls like to be asked."

I could see I wasn't going to win this one and, not wanting to live my entire life with this deep regret that my own Mama had hoisted on me, I went over to Julie Minter in the hall at school the next day and said "Hi, Julie."

She smiled real quick and said "Hi, Compton. How're you doing?"

"I'm fine," I said. "Would you like to go to the Prom?"

"I'd love to," she said, still smiling. "Thanks for asking me." I started to say that I thought Charlene had already asked you but for some reason I didn't, which was probably a good thing.

Well, now I had to rent a tux with a white coat and then buy a corsage cause Charlene insisted it was something I had to do, then I spent the Saturday afternoon of the Prom scared to death I was going to get a phone call asking me to play at a dance somewhere, but that never happened.

I'd never worn a tuxedo before so I had no idea what to do with the cumberbund. I couldn't imagine where it went so I put it on first, like it was a girdle under my clothes, then I put everything else on. I took the corsage out of the refrigerator and drove over to the Minter's and picked up Julie and I could tell she was nervous. I was too. As a matter of fact,

I was scared to death. Her parents were real nice, though, all smiling and took our picture about ten times, then we got in the car and drove to the Prom.

I don't know why I would have regretted missing this Prom my whole life. The band wasn't that good. Julie and I danced but the whole time I wished I was up on the bandstand. We had our picture made and then at midnight we danced a waltz and I took her home and was glad it was all over, which is not to say I didn't have a good time with Julie. There was plenty of people to talk to during the breaks and when the band played they was too loud for anybody to talk, which suited me fine. Julie smiled a lot the whole evening.

The whole next week Mama kept saying, "You and Julie getting married?" Aunt Tootie kept asking "Do you think it'll be a boy or a girl" then she'd laugh her head off. Then there was Daddy saying over and over "That outfit you had on was about as useless as ketchup on green beans" and "You wouldn't want to feed hogs or plow a field in that outfit."

I suppose that evening with Julie Minter should be a bigger deal than I've made it out to be because that was my entire dating life in high school, but there wasn't much to it, really, except that I did see Kathleen Holt there and she smiled at me and waved and said "You look nice, tonight, Compton." I knew that. Much as that outfit cost I'd better look nice.

The one thing the Prom did for me was show me a new song. The guitar player did "Lady of Spain" and I vowed to learn that song so as soon as I got back home after taking Julie to her house I got out my guitar and started working on it. I learned that song pretty quick.

On the next to last day of school we had a Talent Show. I didn't sign up or nothing but one of the teachers, Mr. Goldsmith, asked me if I'd play and sing some songs. I was surprised anybody'd ask. I hadn't planned on doing anything for the Talent Show except watch it but I said "yeah" and he said, "We'd like for you to do three songs at the end of the program. Would that be all right?"

I said, yes, that would be just fine, then I asked him if there was any particular songs he wanted me to do. He said he especially liked "Danny Boy" and I said that was fine. I didn't have the heart to tell him that was Ardmore's song but, then again, the Golden Melody Boys weren't a band anymore.

I'd played that coffee house for three straight weekends and I still played at home by myself, but none of that was the same. That coffee house was a whole world all its own and it was like being on a different planet than in a gym with high school kids. The only connection I really had with my own classmates came when Nimrod Carlton called me up one day and asked if I'd give him some guitar lessons. I'd never given anybody guitar lessons before and I told him that but he said I knew more than he did so any lessons at all would be appreciated. Plus he'd pay me $5 a lesson, so I said all right.

Aunt Tootie always said that the Carltons weren't rowing with both oars in the water and that Nimrod himself wasn't even in the same boat. She said every time she saw somebody in a little white suit she figured they were going down to get Nimrod cause most of the time he was off his rocket. So I should've known better than to even try to give him guitar lessons, but that five dollar bill in front of my nose cut off my good sense.

When I got to Nimrod's house he was dressed up in a brand new black cowboy outfit. He had on a black cowboy hat, a black cowboy shirt with those little pockets that slant up and it was all trimmed in white piping. His pants were trimmed in white piping too and they was tucked inside his cowboy boots, which were red with a white eagle on the front and back. He had on spurs and a big belt that had silver studs all the way around it and a buckle that must've been eight inches wide and six inches tall.

Soon as I got there Nimrod asked me to show him a chord and I showed him the D chord. He put his fingers where I showed him, then walked over to a full length mirror on the wall, looked at himself in the mirror, and started flailing that guitar with his fingers somewhat in the D chord position. It sounded like hell.

I waited for him to come back so I could show him another chord but he never did. Nimrod was happy knowing just one chord and playing it dressed up in his cowboy outfit standing in front of that mirror. I thought that if he ever learned how to play then him and Ardmore Pinworth could be in the same band. Maybe he could just invite Armore over and they'd both stand in front of that mirror.

I stayed at Nimrod's house for about an hour but, aside from showing him that one chord, all I did was sit there. He was happy, though. I wanted to get my five dollars but I never did. I just got tired of being around him and left. By the end of that hour it was a relief to get away. I might've even paid five dollars to get out of there. Looking at it that way, I broke even.

There were twelve acts on the Talent Show and they all had to audition to get on. I was the thirteenth and considered the "featured performer," which means I couldn't win any of the prizes. I sang two songs that Billy Boy used to sing, the Hank Williams song "Hey, Good Lookin'," the Lefty Frizzell song, "Saginaw, Michigan," and then I finished with "Danny Boy." People clapped polite after the first two songs but after "Danny Boy" they really went wild. Course I pulled out all the stops on that one, holding notes twice as long as they shoulda been held and going into falsetto. I used every trick in the book and they all worked.

Forty-Six

School finished up last Friday and the graduation ceremony was last Saturday night. It all went pretty well except Tommy Junior Morgan walked out during rehearsals cause he said he wasn't going to walk in with a nigger. He had to walk beside Janice Alvey, who was actually pretty nice. She ended up walking by herself.

What happened was that we walked in by two's and then split when we got to the front of the auditorium so we ended up sitting in alphabetical order. Tommy Junior thought he was safe cause there wasn't any colored in front or behind him in the alphabet but then they had us paired up with the other end of the alphabet so Tommy Junior never came to graduation.

Mama and Daddy came but Mama forgot the camera and that bothered her. I wasn't so sure I wanted a picture of me in that black robe and square board hat with the tassle get-up. Daddy wore a suit. He looked like it made him suffer. Mama just said, "Do you feel any smarter now that you've graduated?" but before I could answer Daddy said, "Don't be thinking you're different now just because you got that diploma. You need to always remember where you came from and don't get the big head." I almost said that the last time I got the big head it came from moonshine and not a diploma but that would a been smart aleck so I didn't say it. I knew Daddy only finished the eighth grade but he'd done all right so maybe that's why he said that.

Right after the graduation ceremony there was a party for everybody at the Yorkshire Club. That was a fancy place where we weren't usually allowed to go but Kevin Farnsworth's dad was president of the club or something—and Kevin was president of the senior class—so the graduating class got to hold their party there. There was free beer so I took one and sat at a table watching people dance and then Kathleen Holt came over and sat down beside me.

"How're you doing, Compton?" she asked.

I wasn't sure what to say. Here was the girl of my dreams talking to me, but I said, "Fine. How about you Kathleen?"

"Fine," she said. "But I think I'm going to miss my classmates. Aren't you?"

"I don't think so," I said. "I haven't gotten to know a lot of them real good. Especially with all the new people from the other high schools."

"Oh, I know, Compton. I feel the same way. So many new people and it's just so hard to get to know them all in only one year. But I've enjoyed the people I have gotten to know and who knows? Maybe I'll see some after graduation."

I just nodded and said, "Yea, maybe we'll run into these folks again sometime."

Then she said, "Compton, have you decided what you're going to do after you graduate?"

That one caught me by surprise. "No, I haven't," I said. "I guess it's either the Army or college. I haven't decided which. How about you?"

"I'm going to college. William and Mary."

There was a pause.

"I've heard you're quite a singer and guitar player, Compton. Actually, that's not exactly right because I've heard you myself and you are quite a singer and guitar player. Are you going to get in another band sometime?"

"Well, I used to be in a band once," I said.

"Oh, I know. The Golden Melody Boys. I heard they were very good. Especially you, Compton. Weren't you the main guitar player?"

"Yea," I said. I was amazed she knew all this. "And I sang some too."

"Oh, I've heard you sing, Compton. I'm not surprised you sang with the band. You're good enough to be professional. Have you ever thought about that?"

I couldn't believe I was having this conversation. I couldn't decide whether to tell her the truth or not but finally I said, "Yea, I've thought about it. But I don't know if I'll make it or not."

"I think you'll make it," she said, and I felt warm all over. "You've got more talent than anybody I know. With that much talent, you've got to make it. I just know you will."

"Well, thanks," I said. "I appreciate you saying that."

"I said it because it's true, Compton," she said. "I believe you'll be a big star some day and I'll be proud to say I knew you when."

I wondered if she'd also admit she turned me down every time I asked her for a date but I didn't say nothing about that.

"Yea, well," I said. "I'm not so sure about all that but I do love to sing."

"I know you do, Compton, and you should never stop singing. I wish you the very best and I hope we can keep in touch."

"I hope so, too," I said, trying to figure out what she meant by that. "And I wish you the best in college."

"Thanks, Compton." She put her hand on my arm. "It's been good seeing you tonight. Maybe we can talk again."

I just nodded yes as she got up and walked over to a crowd of people and started talking to them.

I only stayed at that party a few minutes more and then I left and went home. It's a funny thing, but ever since that night I haven't been in love with Kathleen Holt. Before then, she was always on my mind but ever since that conversation I hardly think of her at all. I never expected true love to evaporate so quickly.

Forty-Seven

Since graduation I've been trying to figure out what I'm gonna do. Actually, I know what I want to do. I want to pack up my guitar and head to Nashville but the Army is drafting guys as fast as they can graduate high school and there's a place called Viet Nam where they're sending 'em. There's no way to ignore the Army now, every decision I make has that hanging over my head. College sounds like a better idea than getting my rear end shot up so I might go there and maybe I can still play some music in college, although I'm not sure college kids care too much for country music.

Actually, when I think about it, I'm not sure I really want to go to college. I applied to the University of Virginia and got accepted but Daddy said "Son, you're not that smart." I told him I was and pointed out my good grades and that other people who didn't do as good in their grades was going.

He just sat there and said "Well, I just don't see you as college material. None of us ever went to college and we done all right." He paused and then he said, "I heard there's people awfully smart in college and they'll make you feel foolish in a hurry. Besides, I don't know how you'd get the money to go."

I just sat there and didn't say nothing. I found out that I'd won a scholarship to another college that I'd applied for in the guidance counselor's office but the counselor called Mama and said she didn't think I was college material so Mama gave back the scholarship without even telling me, then the counselor's son got it. I don't know why Mama did it without telling me except the guidance counselor talked to her a lot and Mama said later that the counselor made a lot of sense so she agreed about giving up the scholarship for me.

I keep wondering if they needed any country music guitar players in the Army but when I asked Uncle Roadkill, who'd been in the Army, he just said they needed fresh meat and a gun would help me more than a guitar when the shooting started. Said all he remembered about music when he was in the Army was marching bands and there wasn't no guitars in those, so I've got to puzzle on all this over the summer and figure out my life. I'd really like some more time to make up my mind but there ain't no time when Uncle Sam's breathing down your neck. You take your time and next thing you know Uncle Sam makes up your mind for you, then there you go toting a gun through the jungle with water up to your arm pits.

College starts in September and here it is June so I've got a little time to think. Actually, I think I'm in love again. But this time it ain't Kathleen Holt; this time I'm in love with a place.

Every time I think about my life all I see is Nashville and all I want to do is grab my guitar and head there. Nashville seems like a beautiful woman to me, and I need to court her. Need to let her know I love her. Nashville is what's on my mind all right but she might as well be a million miles away. In the meantime I'll pull out my guitar and run over a song I just wrote last night.

    Years of frustration
    No light of salvation
    Sun beatin' down on the row that I hoe'd
    I come down a long pike
    Lovin' but not likin'
    Things that taught me all that I know

    Deeper than lost gold
    Sinner and lost soul
    Prayin' for somethin' over and done
    I wore dungarees
    Dreamed overseas
    Takin' on life as a sharecroppers son

I've warmed myself by an old woodstove
I've sweated when July was hot
I've been turned down by the good folks
Tryin' to be something I'm not

Well life is a gamble
And I'm bound to ramble
I want folks to know me and respect what I've done
But no matter where I'm goin'
There's part of me knowin'
That I'll always be a sharecropper's son

Yea, life's biggest battle
Is fattenin' your cattle
Reach for the stars and follow the sun
But there's no escapin'
The roots of your raisin'
And I'll always be a sharecropper's son

Made in the USA
Charleston, SC
02 January 2012